HEMLOCK

ELLE SAMHAIN

The Shintori Chronicles: Book II

Other Novels by Elle Samhain

Aegis: The Shintori Chronicles Book I

Hemlock by Elle Samhain

© 2019 Elle Samhain

ellesamhain@gmail.com

Cover by Elle Samhain

ISBN: 9781070543512

To my mother and father.

I went against every grain possible and still you

loved me fiercely.

CONTENTS

CONTENT WARNINGS

graphic violence

blood

gore

gun violence

monster horror

body horror

mentions of off-page domestic and sexual abuse

mentions of off-page drug use

mentions of off-page parental neglect

death and murder

CHAPTER ONE

JUSTICE

M ud mixed with the blood oozing out of Avery's busted bottom lip as she was dragged across the unforgiving terrain of the earth. Her croaking cries for help were drowned out by the shouting men as they pulled the other end of the rope wrapped tightly around both of her wrists. The villagers of Centralia emerged from their homes to see the Berserker Witch being punished; their expressions turning into sick smiles of joy.

Only hours before they had been ravaged by the Beldam's Legion - the murder of the High Priestess led by Sera. Avery hadn't been quick enough to keep the body count low and she was being dragged off to die. No, that wasn't it; she attracted the deaths like moths to a flame. It wasn't enough to carry souls off to the afterlife as a Reaper, Balthazar made her into a witch so she could bend them to her will. "Necromancer" was the word Moz had used.

"AEGIS!" She shrieked again, hoping the cat would hear her.

He might not have been able to free her on his own, but he could have warned Moz or the other demons. But her familiar was nowhere to be found.

Avery's legs kicked and flailed, desperately trying to anchor herself in place by burying the heels of her boots in the slick mud. She failed to ground herself as her feet were uprooted and carried with the rest of her.

"OWEN!"

Even the solemn revenant that Balthazar had left in her care was absent. *Fucking useless.* She turned her sore neck towards the man carrying her sword on his back. Hemlock. If there was any way she could get it and slice her palm, feed it a blood sacrifice- *these fuckers will pay.* Anger flared her nostrils knowing just what she was capable of, only to be bested by a group of men much taller than her.

Fuck them all, fuck my short stature. Why couldn't Balthazar have also made her five inches taller while he was at it? It would have at least made it harder for the mob to quite literally pick her up off the street from behind.

"String her up there!"

Avery's eyes widened and she struggled to look behind her. She was suddenly dropped to the ground and the impact re-opened the scabs on her scraped cheek. At first she thought they were heading into an open mouth of darkness until the light from a crackling torch revealed the first trunks of the forest.

"Fuckin' ironic," she said out loud with blood dribbling down her chin.

She had survived the perils of the forest only to be dragged back into it with a death sentence. Demons, Reapers, even death by starvation would have been bearable. If she died by the hands of these men, Avery hoped no one would find her body; it would be far too embarrassing.

The mob stopped at the foot of a large oak and a man closed a grubby fist around the collar of Avery's cloak to pull her up to her feet. She choked on the sudden pressure around her windpipe and he grinned at her with half-rotted teeth before shoving her towards the tree. A much leaner man, perhaps not even much older than she was, took the end of the ropes and tossed it over a low-hanging limb of the tree. Other hands joined him, using all their weight to pull backwards and lift Avery off her feet. Her wrists crunched with pain and she wailed in agony.

"Douse 'er!"

Maurice, the drunkard Moz had lifted money from the night before, stepped forward and began flinging a dark bottle to splash Avery with its contents. A sickly-sweet scent of alcohol curled around her nostrils and her eyes bugged out of her skull with panic.

"LET ME GO!"

She thrashed as hard as she could, hoping that the ropes would break under the strain of her weight. Instead of a captive about to break free, she felt more like a flopping fish pulled out of the sea and dangled like a prize.

"If you don't let me go NOW, you'll get my boot so far up your ass, you'll be tying my shoelaces with your tongue!"

As the largest of the men held the other end of the ropes, the others closed in around her, drawing nearer and nearer with their torches. Her blood was boiling from the heat and she squeezed her eyes shut as she waited for her fiery end.

The air split with a loud crack that echoed off the trees, followed by a heavy squish on the muddy earth. Avery fell hard to the ground when the rope was suddenly slackened, slipping face first in the slick muck. She lifted her head and saw the man keeping the rope was now on the ground, the side of his head completely gone as he lay in a puddle of gory matter and blood. Avery thrashed her head about, looking for the source of the gunshot before scrambling to her feet with her wrists still tied.

"Ave!"

She squinted her eyes until she saw the blonde giant emerge from the misty darkness. Tristan! Avery ran towards him as he knocked away villagers with his weighty arm.

"Cut me free!"

Alice pushed through first, her handgun held up as she herded the crowd of men out of the way. Behind her was Maria with her bow and decorated arrow pulled back, an angry scowl twisted on her copper face. They found the man who had Hemlock strapped to his back and Alice jammed the barrel of her gun into the base of his throat.

"Hand it over, shit sack."

A man lurched towards Alice from behind with his hands raised to grab her gun and Maria's arrow soared into the flesh of his bicep. The man howled, looking from Maria to the feathered arrow with a look of utter fright.

"Stay back, I won't give you another warning!"

He retreated, holding his torch in front of him as though to blind her path for any other incoming arrows.

The man with the gun jabbed in his collarbone didn't have to think twice before scrambling to get Hemlock off his back, flinching when Alice let it dig between the bones as he moved. He dumped the sword onto the ground before stepping away, a childish grin was painted on Alice's face.

"BANG!"

He stumbled backwards, falling onto his hands and knees as he slipped in the slick mud. Alice cackled hysterically, the lilac buns of hair on top of her head bobbing as the frightened man scrambled away.

Tristan ran to Avery, pulling a knife from his belt to saw her free. Alice handed Hemlock over to Maria, who hurried it over to Avery. She fumbled with aching hands as she drew the sword, cutting open her palm. Her blood dribbled down the blade and beaded onto the hilt. The leathery flesh shifted, revealing the single golden eye on the hilt. Hemlock awakened with the taste of her blood sacrifice.

Avery's eyes glazed over white; Hemlock's dark revenants rose with her out of the alcohol-soaked mud. The brown tendrils of her hair lifted as did her sword, not in revenge but in a threat.

"Heed my warning," she spoke to the men who remained, their own blades drawn. "Next time I am crossed, it will be more than just one of you who loses his life."

The revenants itched to cut, to break bones; but Avery never let them out of her grip. Their waiting shadows were enough to inspire fear in the villagers as they fled, leaving behind the corpse of their friend as the last flame of their torches disappeared behind the hill.

Avery felt her shoulders drop in relief as she sighed. Her eyes adjusted to the dark and she heard Maria putting an arrow back in her quiver. Light washed over them as Tristan struck a match, lighting a lantern that he kept hooked to his rucksack.

"How did you find me?"

"Mori. And your screaming," Alice said, pointing towards the patch of flattened grass Avery had not noticed before. The snake was coiled on the ground, perhaps staying out of the way to avoid being trampled in the chaos. Though Alice's familiar still made her nervous, Avery nodded towards her in thanks.

"I don't know what happened," Avery murmured. "I thought it was safe enough to walk alone in town, but I guess...."

She trailed off when Maria threw herself around Avery in a hug. Maria squeezed her once in a tight grip before she stepped back and swatted at Avery's clothes as though her hands would waft away the smell of alcohol splashed on them.

"I'm so glad we found you! You sure do reek, though."

Tristan's giant hand closed around her left shoulder and gave a gentle squeeze once before dropping it. "Ave, can y'do something for me? Let's not tell Moz about this, aye?"

Avery looked up at Tristan, his usually jubilant blue eyes shaded dark as he made the request. The stern tone startled her and she shifted her weight, discomforted by his eerie seriousness.

"Why not?"

"Nora. He can't go through that again, especially not now," he spoke softly.

Of course, Tristan was the one who explained to her about Nora, a witch who was close with Moz in the past. Avery assumed Moz did not tell the story because of his agitation at the time, but maybe it had been out of sheer hurt. His friend was left to die hanging in the trees and he couldn't save her. Even though she didn't think she knew Moz very well, Avery understood how that could open an old wound.

"I won't say anything, I promise."

A lipped grin spread across his face as he nodded once, trusting her answer.

None of them spoke for several minutes as they trudged through the drying mud back to town. Not even the usually-chatty Maria dared to talk about what they had just seen. The squish of the earth under their boots was the only sign remaining of the demon they encountered hours before; Moz soaked the land in a monsoon when he shifted into the Knight of Od whose domain ruled over water.

The lanterns of the town floated into view and the reek of death followed soon after. Avery noticed Maria grip her bow a little tighter, the discomfort visible on her face before she spoke.

"The leeches have flocked here," she whispered as though she was afraid the shadows still lurking around Centralia's darkest corners might hear her. "Nobody goes anywhere alone again, okay? Not until we can consecrate everyone else's sword."

Avery had only encountered them once before, but she was surprised to hear Maria use the same name for the creatures as Moz had spat before with such disgust. The harmless black orbs she saw everywhere in Ardua were demons waiting to grow into humanoid shadows and pounce on despaired souls.

She remembered the piercing white eyes in their bodies of mere shadow, the bubbling burn of their grip. When a living soul was possessed, they became monsters, much like the one that attacked Avery in the forest outside of Ardua. The possessed man was long beyond the stage of being a mere shadow and had nearly killed her with his monstrous claws.

"What do you mean consecrate the swords?"

"Moz's sword was blessed by the High Priestess," Tristan explained. "I wasn't allowed in the ceremony, but an offering was made to Onja, Goddess of Victory."

"Onja certainly has an altar nearby, does she not?" Alice's eyes swiveled side to side as she scanned the main avenue before they entered. "It's not as holy as having it performed by the High Priestess, but should it still work? I'm not quite ready to trust Moz with defending all of us."

Avery thought of his white sword cutting through the Leeches, making their shadows corporeal as their blood seeped inky black. She knew she shouldn't have taken it personally, but Alice's words stung her. Moz could clearly separate himself from the Knight of Od he harbored and had proved it every time he slayed a demon.

"There's no altar dedicated to Onja anywhere near here. We wouldn't be able to do one without either the altar or the High Priestess."

"From what you've all told me," Avery cut in "they're attracted to fear and panic. The best we can do right now might just be to keep calm."

"Wow, gee, I never thought of that. Thanks, Avery," Alice snapped sarcastically.

Avery turned her head to glare; her own point only proven by Alice's quick reaction as a blur of shadows shifted in the swirling reflections on the shop windows. By the time she whirled around with her handgun aimed in the direction of the moving darkness, they were left in the stillness of the early morning once again.

"Avery?"

Avery barely heard Maria behind her when she called out in an unusually soft voice. She whirled around to face Maria's look of unease. Maria's dark eyes slid from the unoccupied house on their side of the avenue to meet Avery's stare.

"What do you suppose happens when the spirits you call up try to fight the Leeches?"

"I'm not sure," Avery admitted. "I've never been able to try, but I'd rather wait until we can get Moz behind us just in case it doesn't work."

That was a question to save for Owen, whenever he returned. Did Balthazar know that the spirit he sent to look after Avery was constantly disappearing? Where did the kid even go to?

She fumbled with the brass chain around her neck for the looking glass Balthazar had given her until she felt the bird skull ornament underneath her fingers. Lifting it up, she peered around the avenue. Her view didn't change, as she had no need for the glass any longer; she could see the spirits without it now.

The only indication that the woman wasn't alive was the faint glimmer of white that trailed behind her when she dashed across the avenue and out of sight. Avery looked at her companions for a reaction to the fast-moving villager, and found they were still scanning the other directions. She knew they weren't going to see the woman, but she still had a difficult time believing that it was her ability alone.

"The best we can do right now is make sure everyone is indoors," Maria suggested. "Both with the Leeches and the possibility Morgana's troops will strike again."

Alice nodded. "Avery and I will search west of here. You and Tristan take to the east. Stick together and we'll meet back here at sunrise. We'll assume something went wrong if you aren't here."

Tristan nodded. "Good plan. Let's go, Maria."

Alice began walking in the opposite direction, motioning with her hand for Avery to follow. "C'mon, Avery. Keep your eyes peeled. If you see a Leech, we've got no choice but to book it outta here."

She reluctantly followed the lilac-haired woman, unsure if she should be relieved or concerned that the one with the guns was eager to pair herself with Avery.

They treaded quietly towards the western flank of Centralia, neither of them speaking a word for the longest time as they kept their cautious gazes moving side to side. They didn't come across a single soul, not even the smallest flicker of life - or afterlife, for Avery. Confusion arose when they began to see shopfronts that were not just abandoned, but their windows and doorways were boarded up.

Avery stopped in front of one shop that looked to be a clothing outfitter, Franklin's Leatherworks, as she was unable to peer through the boarded window. Looking up, she noticed the second-story windows had been blocked off with wood planks as well. Why board up the windows that high up from the street level?

"A lot of businesses have homes on the top floor, where the owners and their families live," Alice explained from where she had stopped a few yards ahead of Avery.

She took one last glance before turning to keep walking after Alice.

"I spoke to Kurosaki," Alice said without turning around towards her and Avery waited for the rest of what she had to say, but the young woman seemed to want Avery to ask instead.

"And?"

"We are choosing not to harm Moz. Not now, and not when this is all over. If he finishes this alive, that is."

"Why, how utterly gracious of you," Avery muttered under her breath. Alice either didn't hear her or chose to ignore the annoyed comment altogether.

She watched Alice ahead of her as she slowly swung her lifted gun side to side as they walked. Alice was always ready to fire shots, no matter the situation.

"Will that gun even do anything against a demon? Or a Leech-whatever?"

Alice shook her head, the lavender buns of hair wagging on the top of her head.

"Scare the shit out of one? Hopefully. Injure one? Likely not. Some people in Eyon have blessed bullets. But they're hard to come by and we didn't get so lucky," Alice answered, climbing over a stack of crates that blocked the alley they cut through. The thud of her boots on the wood sent several black orbs scurrying out from the crevices, Avery watched them flee before she swung her legs over to follow.

"Yeah, I guess it would be hard when you're so secluded from the rest of the continent and didn't have an altar to Onja. How did you and Kurosaki get sucked into this, anyhow?"

"I've known Kurosaki since before we were both Reapers, both just empty children with no souls inside yet. We both had Inception so close together in time and place that we had a strange and vague friendship before he left Eyon."

Empty children with no souls inside. The words felt like a punch to the gut and flickers of facial fragments glittered in her mind's eye. It hurt, so she swallowed the thought away.

"Where did he go?"

"With Moz. He was looking for Reapers in every city he could find. No one in Eyon cared to go with him, no Reaper would listen to his pleas. To this day I'm still not sure if they didn't believe his claims about the Knights or if they're simply too cut off from the world to see it as their problem too. But Izaya believed.

"They were gone for two years, going from Eyon to Wrencrest, up the eastern coast to Ardua. From there through Centralia to Brightloch and making the circuit all around again, looking for anyone who would help them. Then one day Kuro was at my doorstep, telling me that a member of the Beldam's Legion had singled him out for murder. He begged for my help and I couldn't say no, not after everything."

"The last Knight hadn't been placed at this time, but we knew it was coming. We scraped up as many Reapers as we could - we had a whole outpost just outside of Brightloch. But as time passed, they were unconvinced that the Beldam was really a threat. Then it was just us, most recently you."

Something about the way Alice said the words translated into a sentiment that Avery didn't belong there. Did she mean it or was Avery taking it too hard?

Avery found her footsteps had fallen slower as her feelings of doubt thickened and she hurried to catch up with the leather-clad woman. A couple of hours had passed and still they had yet to encounter another villager.

"I don't think there's a single person out here," Alice said and stopped in the middle of the road, looking in all directions with her gun lowered at her side. Ahead of them, the buildings were beginning to dissolve into field as they neared the western edge of Centralia.

"Can we risk making that assumption?" Avery asked.

"We're gonna have to, the sun is rising."

Alice turned on her heel, wasting no time in heading back in the direction where the sky burned early orange. They retraced the path they had already taken with hasty footsteps, not meticulous or the least bit careful in scanning the same places again.

The tall shape of Tristan came into view at the end of the street, the small form of Maria right beside him. Even from where they waited, Avery could point out which of the two of them was the most nervous; Maria's bow darting in every direction as they passed pathways.

"Ah, there they are," Alice said and stood up. "I was beginning to worry."

CHAPTER TWO
THE HERMIT

Shank was the first to emerge from the healer's house as they rubbed the last hints of sleepiness away from their eyes. Avery eagerly stood up from the ground where she had sat to wait, shaking off her own weariness as subtly as she could.

"How is he?"

They let out a sharp sigh, worrying Avery until she remembered Maria mentioning they did that no matter the situation.

"Unsurprisingly, he's not talking much. No doubt he's still scared of what we might do. But he's on his way up, Jane's just getting one last look at him before she lets him go. Wait here just a little bit longer and we'll take him home."

At the mention of Jane's name, Avery looked down at where Maria still sat on the ground. She was met with a look of revulsion as she shook her head and Avery knew exactly why. The halo of white orbs that surrounded Jane the night before and the chimes that only Avery had heard; she was supposed to Reap Jane. When Avery had mentioned it to Maria at Moz's bedside she had seemed already overcome with grief for the old woman. Avery sank back down to the ground, remembering the look.

How was Avery going to Reap her? Her method in Ardua was simply touching the stranger, pretending she was someone they might have encountered on any ordinary day. Taking even strangers to their death took a toll on her well-being, but this was someone she had spoken to and knew - even if only on the smallest basis. She had also probably saved Moz's life. Why did that small fact matter at all to Avery?

The tall figure emerged from the doorway, ducking under the frame. His hard jaw was clenched to hold his mouth in a firm line. Sleep was heavy on the bottom shadows of his eyes, too fatigued to hold their characteristic anger. The longer tendrils of dark hair on the top of his head were astray in every direction and made the weariness in his face all the more obvious. Avery stood up shortly after Maria did.

"How do you feel, Moz?"

He looked at Avery before answering, the green of his eyes seeming to slowly flicker back to life. He frowned, perhaps wondering why Avery was the only person whose clothes were coated in a thick layer of dried mud, but he made no relevant remark.

"Like someone's been redecorating my insides."

She let herself exhale in relief, glad to know that a grueling night of injury treatment didn't take away from his humor. Maria stepped forward with her arms raising as though to hug him but stopped when she thought better of it and put her arms back down. It was likely best not to hug someone with a nasty shoulder wound.

"Let's get you home," she offered instead.

Moz turned and looked back towards the door as though he wasn't sure if he could leave just yet. The spotted white rat that had been burrowed in the hood of his coat peeked over his shoulder and Avery smiled at the cheery sight of Jack.

"Yeah, let's go," he said. He began to follow Shank towards the direction of the shack, Maria trailing behind them. "C'mon, Avery."

Maria stopped and looked over her shoulder at where Avery was still standing. Her expression was solemn; she knew exactly why Avery lingered at Jane's door.

"I'll catch up," Avery called out after them.

Maria hesitated before turning to catch up to the two men. When they had vanished, Avery sucked in a deep breath; there were no excuses to stall left anymore. She stared at the peeling mint paint of the front door before pushing it open again.

The inside of the healer's home remained dim with no windows to let in the morning sunlight. Her boots creaked the tired floorboards, but the elderly woman still stood with her back to Avery, paying no mind to her unexpected return. The cot Moz had laid in the night before was made neatly and the blood-soiled linens were already replaced.

Jane uncorked glass vials and peered inside to assess their contents before capping them, putting them inside a wooden box. She still did not acknowledge Avery - perhaps she somehow did not hear her walk inside?

White orbs still floated around the woman's head, the mark of death that said Jane was the next to be sent to the afterlife. Avery knew that Jane's name also would have been in the black ledger given to her by whoever made her a Reaper, but she did not dare to open the book ever since she had left Ardua.

"I know why you're here," Jane said simply before Avery could announce herself.

"You do?"

"You're not a local. It's easy to tell," the old woman explained. "But around here, folks are devout. We believe the legends. The Beldam, the gods, the Reapers, all of them. It looks like now I get to know for sure, isn't that right?"

The chuckle Jane gave could have held either relief or sadness, Avery wasn't sure. She stood in the dim room, unsure of how she was supposed to react to a human who knew what was about to happen to them. What little de-briefing she had during her Inception mentioned no such thing happening.

"You understand that you're going to die?"

Jane nodded, setting down the cloth that she had just finished folding. She turned to face Avery, her mouth smiled knowingly and the folds of her age-spotted face wrinkling in places that made it clear this woman had spent most of her life grinning.

"I don't think we're given enough credit, us ordinary folk."

Sadness washed over Avery in a tidal wave and she reeled backwards as though getting away from this woman would prevent her from having to send Jane to her death. Jane's glance turned skeptical, like she hadn't expected her Reaper to be so emotional.

"If I can just say something first," Avery sputtered. "I really don't want to do this. And not just because you saved Moz, I mean, that means a lot to me, but I can't do this. Not without knowing where I'm sending you."

Jane smiled sweetly and put down the antiseptic bottle she was holding, putting both of her hands on Avery's shoulders to look up at her. Horror flooded Avery when she realized just how content this woman was with death.

"Honey," Jane spoke with a velvet soft voice. "I've outlived both my husband and my only daughter. I've come to that temple every day to tell the Goddess how much I love Her even despite the fact She has taken what I treasure most. I'm not afraid. Not of death and certainly not of you."

Avery wanted to argue but she was frozen in stunned fear. The woman had taken her by the hands - a touch of the skin was what Avery used to mark them for death. What would happen when one of the Marked had touched *her*?

"Now I'm very tired," Jane continued, the touch seeming to have no effect on her beating heart. "I spent all night helping your friend and now that he is alright, I may rest. If it is okay, I would like for you to wait until I'm already asleep."

She nodded after attempting to choke out verbal approval and Jane smiled. The old woman turned around, smoothing out the cot with her hands before sitting on the edge.

"You know, I think in life we could have been friends," Jane said warmly, only adding to Avery's terror. Was the woman making this difficult for her on purpose?

"I would have liked that."

The old healer smiled once more and laid on her back, folding her fingers together patiently on her sternum with closed eyes. She then chuckled to herself, her shoulders wiggling.

"You'll know I'm asleep when I start snoring, Arthur always said it was terrible."

Avery nodded even though Jane would not have seen, and she sank back into the shadowy corner of the small room, waiting with a bit lip to hold back cries of guilt. Why was the old woman okay with dying this way?

Silence settled over the room like dust. A small stirring came from underneath the bed and Avery jumped backwards against the wall in fright. Candlelight reflected on small marble-like orbs as a shadow slinked out from beneath the cot.

"I think she's asleep now."

Avery puffed out her cheeks to keep herself from yelling out in anger at Aegis.

"Wherehaveyoubeen," she hissed her sentence in a single word, trying not to awake Jane.

"With Moz. I wanted to poke at the Knight a bit. I needed to know why the demon lured you in back there in the field. I'll explain later."

She had so much she could have asked her familiar right then, but she knew she needed to keep quiet. Avery stepped forward, ignoring the cat, and leaned over where Jane lay on the cot. She watched with trembling focus, trying to determine if the movements of the old woman's chest could signify sleep. Avery raised her fingers just above Jane's mouth, taking great care to avoid touching her skin. Warm, steady bursts of air from the woman's nostrils wrapped around Avery's fingers. Jane's exhales were deep and slow; she was certainly asleep.

Avery slowly moved her shaking hand and gently touched Jane's cheek. At first, she thought nothing had changed until the white orbs began to fade out of her vision. The gentle movement of Jane's chest subsided as she took her last breaths. She became still, and then she was gone.

Avery stood over Jane's peaceful body, her vision becoming blurry as her eyes welled with tears. This woman just saved Moz and she was only rewarded with death.

"You have always struggled bringing them to me, daughter," a velvet-soft voice spoke behind her. "What a gift you had given her, to go so peacefully in a dream."

She turned her head over her shoulder only far enough to see the figure who had appeared and consumed the corner of the room with its looming presence. Balthazar.

"So... many people have died by my hand," she choked. "I can't do this anymore. I can't be a Reaper, take it back."

Balthazar shook his head, clicking his tongue twice on the roof of his mouth in exaggerated pity.

"You can renounce your Reaperdom all you want; it won't change a thing. If Beldam hasn't yet set her sights on killing you, she will if you refuse to carry out her wishes."

How could this be? Avery couldn't hide the pleading in her eyes as she waited for him to make an amendment to the bad news. She turned her head back to Jane's deathbed to hide the tears that were beginning to slip from the rim of her eyes; she couldn't barter if she was sobbing.

"But your wife is Queen of the Witches, she can do anything."

"You're right, she can do anything," she didn't have to be facing the Keeper of the Crossroads to hear the proud smile in his tone. "Though that is something outside of her means not because of ability, but conflict within the family of the gods."

Family of the gods. The mysterious elite that intervened in human activity only when they wanted to satiate their boredom or needed hands dirtied. Avery twitched in recoil at the violent realization and her grief became enflamed rage.

"You're using us… all of us, to settle a petty score," she hissed.

"I never pretended that we weren't," he said simply. "Reapers are tools of the gods by purpose and nature."

Her blood boiled and her fingernails dug into the palms of her hands as her stance went rigid. "Get out of my sight, leave me alone."

Avery wouldn't have dared speak in such a way if he was a god, she had to remember what he was. A demon and nothing more; no worse and no better than the Knight of Od that Moz harbored. His expression did not change, the deep flesh of his face did not shift in any way to indicate anger at her demand.

"Avery Porter, do you even know how you're going to eliminate the Knights once you arrive at Eyon?"

The Priestess. Avery heard the whistling of Sera's poison arrow soaring past her ear and lodging into her chest as she instructed them. How could she have been so fucking stupid? They had no idea what to do once they arrived at the pit. Somehow, she doubted it was as simple as slitting the palms of a Reaper and a Saved.

"The full ritual is in Mona's spell book. It was stolen by a demon and is in the heart of Od, the Necropolis. I cannot retrieve it because they will be looking for me."

Avery wiped the angry tears off her face. "And you need us to get it?"

"Well, it would appear that it's our only option, doesn't it? If you could put aside your hatred of the gods for a while and do that, I believe it will pay off a thousand-fold," his words held a slight bite that unnerved Avery and she frowned.

"But I can't get to Od, I'm alive."

"Ha!" The sudden jolt of laughter made the heavy air of the room vibrate and Avery flinched. "You can when you're dealing with me. I can very easily place someone living in the land of the dead and the demons. However, the Necropolis is closer to being beneath Brightloch than it is to Centralia and I would like to get you as close as I can to the vault it is being kept in."

Avery stared at him for a moment. "I don't actually have a choice, do I?"

"Not even the illusion of one."

Her jaw hardened and she sucked in a breath through her nose - it was clear that she was going to have to run an errand for Balthazar.

"Then I suppose I'll do it."

The demon of the crossroads grinned with grimy teeth before he vanished, leaving Avery and Aegis alone in the room with Jane's body. She stared at it for a long moment and swore to herself that Jane would be the last to die by her hands, aside from the members of Beldam's

Legion. Avery left the dim room, intentionally leaving the front door open to invite in someone to find the body.

Her footsteps were quick and heavy as she trudged back in the direction of the shack, Aegis silently trailing behind her. It was not until they made it halfway until she found herself composed enough to speak.

"So, what did you find out while you were grilling poor Moz?"

"Well as I had suspected, he had no say in the Knight luring you or any idea why it listened to you. But I am very surprised to say that he is an incredibly guilt-ridden bastard. No need to look there for his hidden emotion."

Avery was taken aback. "Guilt? But why?"

"It's hard to say. Severely underestimating you, the Knight luring the person who knew him the least, not saying something to give anyone time to flee, being a generally cruel person. It could be anything, really."

"I think his apology was sincere. Only time will tell, though."

"He knew of no motive for the Knight luring you. But I do."

Avery froze, watching the cat trot ahead of her. Realizing she had stopped, he looked at her over his haunches with a swishing tail.

"Why?"

"The Knights wish to emulate Balthazar and Mona, though why I cannot be certain. My theory is their twisted minds think it will grant them good standing with the gods if, like Balthazar, they attach themselves to a witch."

"Wh... what? That's ridiculous! I don't want to-"

"It's platonic. What are you, five?"

Not waiting for her to answer, Aegis resumed forward on their path back to the shack. Avery was slow to follow, trying to understand the demon guide's reasoning.

"Why would they want to be in good standing with the gods? They're already trying to tear everything down," she said as she jogged to catch up to Aegis, slowing down beside him.

"How should I know? Ask Bone Brain."

After they reached the haphazardly constructed shack, Aegis darted ahead of her and looked back.

"Rid yourself of the mud before tracking it in someone else's home. Let's try to have at least some sense of decency."

Before she could laugh and offer up a scathing rebuttal along the lines of him leaving her for dead, the demon familiar slunk inside and left Avery alone.

Stopping feet from the wall of the shack, she stood still in the quiet field - waiting. When was the next time she would be preyed upon by the mortals who didn't know any better? She hardly thought that their one failed attempt would be enough to deter them from trying to slay the Berserker Witch again. Not after what it appeared she was responsible for. If she had refrained from assaulting the men on her first night in Centralia, she might not have found herself the scapegoat for the mass slaughter.

Was anyone even able to make the connection between Moz and the sapphire beast that terrorized the skies just the previous night? That might have been a stretch considering the Reapers were the only ones in that field; they had seen Avery's pull over the dead with their own eyes. A pang of shame hit Avery for tangentially wishing her fate had fallen upon Moz.

"He doesn't deserve it either," she muttered to herself, as though saying the words out loud made it easier to forgive the thought.

She watched the forest just over the hill as it swayed in the wind, the dull roar of blowing leaves was the only sound heard over the muffled voices of her friends coming from inside. There was no one to be seen amongst the trees before she disappeared around the corner of the shack. Though she was mostly confident she was alone, she hurried when turning on the faucet, scraping clumps of mud away from her skin with her fingernails as quickly as she could.

At the unexpected whinny of a horse from within the nearby stables, she jumped into startled action as she turned off the faucet and ran inside. She leaned against the closed door, making a conscious effort to slow her frightened heart. When she felt calm again, she walked into the sitting area to shed her cloak and take off her armor.

"Avery?"

Moz called out her name and she turned around after she finished peeling off her plate of armor. "Yeah?"

He didn't say anything before pulling her into a hug, bending down slightly at the waist to avoid wrapping his arms around her head. She couldn't even twist her face into a look of incredulousness at the bizarreness of the hug. Was this still Moz?

"I can't thank you enough for what happened back there," he said in the held hug. "I'm glad to know I can trust you."

Maybe it wasn't so strange after all. She and Tristan were the only ones who didn't have the initial reaction to try and kill Moz after finding out he was the Knight of Water. Her shoulders relaxed from their reflexive freeze and she smiled.

"Of course."

He let go of her and turned to leave, never catching a glimpse of her smile. The scent of clove and tobacco faded from her nostrils as she found that she had been standing still moments after he left. Nope, still strange.

"Well, that was bizarre," a familiar voice said, and Avery whirled around.

Owen stood halfway in the kitchen, a skeptical smirk on his ghostly face. She knew she should have been angry that he had waited so long to reappear rather than when she was in danger, but she made a conscious effort to let it go.

"How long were you standing there?"

The boy shrugged. "Couple of minutes?"

"Can you do something for us? We found out that the last Knight is in Brightloch– Princess Yumi. Is there any way you can go ahead of us and let her know we're coming? That we'll take her to safety before Morgana reaches her?"

Owen nodded. "I can travel through Od; I could certainly relay the message soon."

Avery's eyes lit up. "Thank you, Owen! Wait, before you go, is it at all possible for you to take something back from Od? To the living?"

His golden eyes narrowed with confusion, his chin tilting away from Avery as though she should have known the obvious answer.

"Not a chance," he said. "The only reason I can manipulate objects here is because of you. I can't feed off you from Od."

"Feed off me," she blurted out - *surely, I had heard him wrong?*

Owen nodded to confirm his choice of words. "I don't see how Hemlock could have been doing anything else with the blood sacrifices you give it."

"Avery, c'mere," Tristan said, the heavy thud of his boots passing through the kitchen behind her. She whirled around to face the large man, tailed by a smaller Shank.

"Shank had a genius idea I reckon we try," he continued as he threw a chair out from underneath a crooked table, the wood creaking under his large frame when he sat down.

In his hands he held what appeared to be a glass capsule and pulled out the cork that sealed its opening. Shank stepped around him to reach for the sagging candle melted to the table, striking a match to light it.

"We need you to test something first," Shank said, looking down at the candle to Avery. "Cut your hand with a dagger and wipe the blood on the leather of Hemlock's hilt."

"What? Why?"

"Well, it would seem that if you're ever separated from Hemlock, you're screwed. But I was curious to see if you need to cut yourself with it, or if you can just get your blood to the sword and be able to call up spirits. Maybe we can even take a piece of leather from the hilt."

She looked from the sheathed sword hanging from the back of the chair to Shank. It seemed crazy, but maybe crazy enough to work. Avery reached for the pile of armor she had shed, knowing her dagger was beneath it - the dagger Moz had given her when she was taken from Ardua.

Avery came back to the table, wincing as she pricked her finger with the dagger; it hurt quite a bit more without the adrenaline rush of battle to dull the sharp pain. When a bead of blood formed on her index finger, she looked at Shank as they carefully stripped part of the dark leather from the handle of Hemlock. After toiling for a few minutes, they placed a small scrap of leather down onto the table.

"Go ahead and smear your finger on that," they instructed.

She nodded and picked up the piece with her unpricked hand, wiping her bleeding finger against the leather. Avery watched Tristan instinctively move his hand to the dagger on his waist as revenants seeped upward through the floorboards. Locks of her dark hair floated up toward the ceiling and the brass-rimmed looking glass around her neck followed. With her eyes fogged over in a milky-white haze, Avery turned to Shank.

"My guess is that it works," she said, her own voice sounding dissonant to her ears. Shank smacked the table with their palm in excitement and Avery flinched at the sharp bang.

"Brilliant!"

They picked up Hemlock again, beginning to cut off more of the brown leather with their pocket knife.

"Now we just need a piece long enough for Avery to wear around her wrist and sew on a capsule filled with blood and water - I'm sorry, but you're going to need to prick your finger again. And then any time you're in trouble, you smash the capsule onto the leather."

When she failed to sic the hungry spirits on a target, they faded from view and gravity worked itself again upon her hair and necklace. She looked at Shank's knife slicing the leather nervously but became more relaxed once she realized nothing adverse was happening.

"It really is brilliant, thank you," she murmured, hesitating before piercing the skin of her left palm. As she hissed in pain before putting down the dagger, the sound of the faucet sputtering water came from the kitchen and Tristan returned with the glass capsule filled halfway with water.

He carefully held the vial between his large thumb and index finger, handing it over to Avery. She held it against her palm, letting the crimson beads fall into the glass and cloud the water red.

She handed the vial to Tristan and traded it for the cotton cloth Shank gave her to staunch the blood from her hand. Avery watched as the exorcist corked the narrow vial and dipped the cork and lip of the glass in the liquid candle wax, turning it slowly to seal the glass all the way around.

"This part will take a bit longer, so please be patient," Shank took the capsule after the wax had dried and she laughed when she saw they had been holding a sewing needle between his teeth.

They began to sew the capsule against the strip of leather, the black thread swallowing up the bottle with each few minutes that passed. As she watched, she found herself entranced and relaxed by the gracefully repetitive movements. She found her head sinking lower, even as it was propped up on her unscathed hand. *Sleepy, so sleepy.*

"Mission accomplished!"

She shot up at the sudden excitement in Shank's voice and they held up the finished bracelet. The blood-filled capsule was completely hidden by the dark thread that held it against the leather.

"Hold out your non-dominant hand," they said and Avery held out her left arm, the blood-stained cloth still crumpled in her fist.

With quick and nimble fingers, Shank looped the leather around her wrist. They spun the bracelet around to tie the ends in a series of knots, gently tugging on it to see if it would hold. When they were satisfied, they looked at Avery with a toothy grin.

"And there you have it!"

Avery twirled her arm around, watching the way it twisted on her wrist. She took the rolled-up end of her sleeve and carefully pulled it over the bracelet, hopefully cushioning the glass even more with the fabric.

"Thanks, Shank."

It was not Avery who had spoken, and she turned in surprise at the sound of Moz's voice from behind them.

The three of them were frozen in place around the small table. Did Moz find out about the witch hunt? His face was solemn, but it was difficult to tell his exhaustion from his stern expression.

"I understand the concern, but I'm not nearly as fragile about Nora as you think I am," Moz continued flatly. "I'd appreciate a level of honesty, at least on the level of demons."

Oh, fuck. Avery realized that he must have heard about the villagers' attempt on her life through one of the familiars; he could talk to all of them.

Her gaze slid to the snake on the floor of the sitting room, watching them with black eyes from where it basked in the sunlight falling in through the colored window. Of course, it was Mori; Alice was there at her rescue and her familiar had no obligations to any of the three of them.

"Moz, I—"

"Like I said, I understood the concern," he cut off Avery's apology. "For now, I'm more worried about getting out of here as soon as possible to head to Brightloch."

Without another word, he disappeared through the front door and left them in a guilty silence. In his absence Avery saw Maria standing in the door frame of her small room with the same sadness painted on her face; Maria had chosen not to tell Moz, either. Instead of speaking she waved Avery over to come in her direction.

"Get a change of clothes before we go; you're a mess," she suggested in a flat voice missing her usual jubilance.

As Avery did only two days before, she rummaged through the dilapidated bureau in the corner of the room. The shirt and pants she picked were both black and perhaps influenced by the dark cloud that hung over the group after Moz's confrontation.

On her way out she picked up the dark green cloak once more. Even though it was sullied by mud, she still felt an attachment. The cloak worn by the Berserker Witch - that's who she was now. With the small click of the clasp closing at the base of her throat, she somehow felt safer.

The house was empty, aside from Mori. Avery pushed open the creaky front door and voices coming from the stable were carried on the breeze. She rounded the house and saw Tristan's large frame standing in the entry to the stable. As she approached, the murmur of their voices grew quieter and she hesitated. Did they not want her to hear?

Tristan looked behind him at Avery and waved her in.

"-I officially have nothing to hide from any of you," Moz was saying as she stepped inside, seeming to finish up whatever they had been discussing. Maria, Shank, Alice, and Kurosaki were all present as well; stuffing objects into bags with looks of shame or embarrassment painted on their faces. She guessed that she had just missed a stern talking-to.

"How does it feel?"

Moz looked over his shoulder at Avery as he stamped out what was left of the roll of tobacco and clove into the dirt. He stood up from the crate he had been straddling.

"It feels good. Damn good."

"Is there really any point to keep on smokin' that?" Tristan asked as he stood up from where he had been bent over his bag, swinging it over his shoulder.

"Now that the Knight broke out, I reckon the clove don't do much."

"Nasty habits die just as nasty, I suppose."

"So, what's our plan," Shank was the first to change the subject to what was certainly more important. "We grab the Princess and take her to Eyon?"

"More or less," Kurosaki said, strapping a black pad to his forearm. "I imagine I need not remind you it's easier said than done. Finding a ship captain willing to go to Eyon will be difficult."

"We'll cross that bridge when we get to it, I reckon," Tristan brushed aside the concern.

Moz appeared to agree with the sentiment, striding to his horse with one open hand held up and his back still to the rest of the Reapers as he instructed "I want to be on the road in five minutes. We must move as quickly as possible."

Five minutes? Avery huffed, they had only just returned and her near-death experience had left her exhausted, to say the least. She watched as he emptied the contents of the black saddle bag on Emory, noticing that he did not replace them.

"Are we not going by horse?"

Moz shook his head. "Not feasible on the terrain we'll have to cross and how much food we'd have to be carrying. Not much use either for when we have to sail across the Stillmaw. A friend, Lenore, will be taking care of them in our absence."

"Are you fucking serious," she couldn't hide her bewilderment and Moz looked back with a raised brow. "By the time we get to Yumi, we'll have crossed nearly the entire continent on foot. That's not 'quickly as possible'."

"Shintori isn't nearly as big as cartographers make it appear on paper," Shank cut in. "Another way of keeping the regions cut off and to themselves. I'd roughly estimate we reach Brightloch in a week, with a good pace of course. That will put us there about a week before the city will be a mess with the Novara equinox festivals."

She still felt skeptical, but also knew she wasn't in a position to argue. Avery pursed her lips and looked from Shank to where Aegis was perched on a stall beam.

"I'll go pack then."

Avery walked out of the stable and back in the direction of the haphazardly constructed house, at first ignoring the footsteps that she swore were following her.

She made it only half the distance when her name was called out from behind her.

"Avery, can I talk to you in private?"

She turned around, stopping as she watched Moz approach her with a rather relaxed posture. Not at all like the tense air he held only moments before.

"Of course," she answered.

He stopped at an arm's reach from her, close enough to see the healing scrape across his cheek and marred brow.

"Are you hurt?"

The question caught her off guard; she hadn't expected Moz to mention the villagers' attack beyond what he had said in the shack. There was nothing beyond scrapes and a scabbed lip, so she shook her head.

"I'm glad," he said. "Look, I meant what I said. I'm not mad about you three trying to hide what happened from me. But you and I both know that the only reason you're here is because I did something fucked up and kept fucking up along the way."

The confusion on her face certainly showed, for he sighed and looked frustrated as though he was mentally backpedaling.

"What I mean is I'm sorry, and I'm going to keep saying sorry," he said. "Because we, I, look at you as a friend. And I don't want you or anyone else to feel like you have to walk on eggshells around me because I'm trying to not be that person anymore. Please just be honest with me because I'm taking so much care to do the same now. I'm sorry."

As Moz spoke he had been looking down at his boots with flickers of anger intended not for her. He couldn't bring himself to make eye contact as he apologized and his self-awareness brought him shame.

"I already said I forgive you, Moz," she tried to keep her words gentle. "You were very clearly dealing with something bigger. I don't think I could have handled it any better if I were in your shoes."

He looked up with the corners of his mouth turned up in a small smile.

"Just promise not to kidnap any more people," she added jokingly.

Instead of answering, he reached a hand into the charcoal cowl that hung loosely around his neck. He pulled out the clapperless bell that hung on a red cord, gently removing it up and over his head. Moz held it in an extended palm to her.

"I want you to have it."

"Moz, no. This means a lot to you and I-"

"It does mean a lot to me. But fixing everything means more."

She hesitated, not sure if she should honor his wish or insist that he keep the treasured object. Avery finally reached out, pulling it delicately from where it sat in his cupped hand.

"Thank you, Moz. I don't really know what to say."

He waved his hand once as though to brush her gratitude aside. "Don't worry about it. Make sure you're ready to go, okay?"

Avery nodded. "I will."

When Moz turned and walked away, Avery looked over at where Owen had watched, completely unseen by Moz. His eyes were wide with confusion, as she imagined hers were.

"Bizarre, indeed," she said.

CHAPTER THREE
THE DEVIL

W here is everyone?"

Avery looked around the cobblestone avenue. Alice was right - the town was eerily empty. Fruit carts stood abandoned with their contents spilled, shop doors were locked, and the windows were darkened if not boarded up. Paired with the spilled blood of villagers still lingering in the crevices of the cobblestone, Avery fixed her mouth in a frown.

"This can't be good," Avery murmured.

As they followed the main avenue deeper through Centralia, the sense of abandonment grew even stronger when they failed to encounter a single human face - she didn't count the ghostly faces she caught ducking around corners to avoid them. Gray rats skittered down alleyways, frightened by the sudden sounds of feet as the band of Reapers passed.

The silence was broken by a loud splintering of wood coming from a parallel vein of town. In front of her, Maria fumbled before raising her bow. Drawing his sword quickly, Moz spun his head and scanned the buildings that flanked them on either side.

"Mr. Mosley!"

An unfamiliar voice called out and Avery followed Moz's gaze to their left, toward a man waving them over from an alleyway. Moz looked behind him at the rest of the group, signaling them to follow with two fingers before striding quickly over to the man. Avery followed closely behind, her right arm reaching over her shoulder to hold the handle of Hemlock in case things went awry.

"Who are you?"

They stopped for the man, Avery and Moz at the head of the group. The man held an uneasy look in his young face, his brow scrunched and lips pursed tight. His brown hair came to the bottom of his earlobes, a scruffy beard covering the bottom half of his face. He wore a sheath at his hip, one end of his brown leather coat bunching under the strap as though he had thrown it on in a panicked hurry. The man's brown eyes looked from Moz to Avery, the visible panic strengthened before darting his gaze back to Moz.

"My- My name is Chauncey Grimmwold. I'm sorry, I didn't realize you had the Berserker Witch with you."

Avery's eyes went wide, stunned by the man's audacity and she began to turn to leave the group.

"You treat her with respect or I'm not bothering to make your acquaintance. How do you know me?"

"I'm sorry," Chauncey said to Moz, sounding more terrified than authentically apologetic. "Just, I know when someone needs something killed, they call Mr. Mosley."

Avery looked up at Moz. "What's he talking about?"

He didn't answer her question, his cold stare fixed on the shorter man. "What's going on? Where is everyone?"

"Hiding. From the demon-beast. There are but a few men wandering, trying to find it and slay it before it can kill anyone else."

Moz looked over his shoulder in the direction of the others. "Leech. Must have snagged someone."

He turned his attention back to Chauncey, who was looking rather perplexed. Avery felt Aegis stir in the hood of her cloak before he spoke to her.

"I must say, now that it's been pointed out I can certainly feel it. Not quite as in-your-face as having Bone Brain over here, but it's there."

Moz flashed a scowl down at the cat, hearing the name-calling as clearly as Avery did, before turning back to the shorter man. "How many people has it killed?"

"Last I got word of - seven."

"We have to help them," Maria said softly from behind them.

Moz turned around, his back to Chauncey in order to deliberate with the rest of the group. The grave expression on his face mirrored in Jack's small face from where he was perched on Moz's shoulder.

"It will set us back, but you're right. We can't just leave them to fend for themselves. Any protests?"

"I don't think any of us are that shitty of people, so we should probably help," Kurosaki said, casting his vote. Moz's gaze slid from Kurosaki and over the faces of the rest of the group to make sure the sentiment was unanimous.

Avery watched as he turned back to Chauncey, lifting his sword once and then back down as though to display that he had decided to aid him.

"Show us the way."

Chauncey had a flash of bewilderment on his face, surprised that Moz had agreed, before nodding and turning down to face the other end of the alley.

"Thank you, Mr. Mosley! Follow me this way!"

Chauncey darted down the alley, disappearing around the corner by the time they started to follow him. They weaved in and out of alleyways, zipping through side avenues. Avery found herself dizzied by the left turns followed by right turns only to turn left twice more.

"Where are we going?" She called out but was doubtful that the man would respond to her and scowled at the thought of the sour reputation that was already preceding her.

"The last sighting was just outside Barnaby's dry goods store," Chauncey called out as though Avery was supposed to know where that was. "Probably gone by now, but it should give us some idea of where it'll go next."

They dashed onto another street, where evidence of the demon began to appear. Avery caught glimpses of splintered doors, gashes cutting into the paneled facades of homes and storefronts as though the creature had forced itself inside. Blood spatter trailed out of one doorway for several feet before disappearing altogether.

"Grimmwold!"

A group of men waved at them from the end of the avenue. Chauncey's face lit up and he sprinted towards them.

"I found help!"

The group of men ran to meet him, a man with long raven hair patting Chauncey on the back with his large palm.

Before the Reapers could even catch up to Chauncey, an explosion of wood from a nearby house sent sharp splinters crashing in every direction. Avery ducked with her forearm held protectively over her eyes, waiting till the clattering of wood on stone stopped to look up.

She saw the swishing tail first, a large horn of black bone jutting out from the end. Its body was scaled as though to be reptilian, but even with its back to her Avery could see the thick fur around where she imagined its head was. Standing on four clawed paws, it ducked its head down from where it towered over the men, closing its teeth down on one of them with a sharp crunch.

"Get it, quick!"

At Shank's command, Maria fired arrows at the beast's back. It whirled its head around, Avery gasping when she looked upon the head of a giant bison. It snarled with rows of jagged teeth, the bones and crevices between them stained crimson. The demon-bison reared back on its hind legs, letting out a piercing screech before launching itself onto the roof of a building to watch them above with a swaying tail.

"It's getting ready to strike again," Moz said, stepping closer to the building with his white sword raised. "Stay as far back as you can."

The demon cried out again before launching itself from the rooftop into the group of men, pinning Chauncey to the ground and knocking his sword out of his shaking hands.

The beast plunged its teeth through Chauncey's gut and his scream echoed off the silent houses. His legs squirmed as though he was still trying to kick the beast off him, his writhing doing nothing to stop the snapping jaws.

"Somebody help him!" Maria cried out. Her arrows hit the demon and lodged into the black scales, but she was powerless to stop it.

Avery was at a loss for how help could be possible. How could Chauncey even still be alive? Beside her, Alice lifted her handgun and two bullets cracked through the air twice before his cries were quieted. Avery buckled at the sound with her hands clamped over her ears. When the ringing in her eardrums stopped, she found that in his silence he left the far more terrible sound of flesh between the gnashing teeth of the demon Alice had not even aimed for. Avery hoped his death was quick and merciful enough.

Moz dashed towards the beast with a raised sword, swiping at air when the demon left his prey to evade the quick attack.

"You'll get your answer now, Alice," Avery mumbled with no intention of Alice hearing her, slicing open her palm with the edge of Hemlock.

The spirits seeped upwards from the ground as slithering shadows - and then hesitated.

"Oh shit, shit, shit," Avery stammered in terror, backing away.

Just when she was certain that the spirits would make no attempt to even confront the demon-beast, they were picking up splintered wood and hurling projectiles at it from an unusual distance. She couldn't help but notice that they never dared to come close to the beast as it sparred with Moz.

A board left the fingers of an angry revenant, nearly clipping the top of Moz's head before he had managed to duck out of the way.

"DO YOU MIND," he shouted in frustration, leaving a second long enough for the demon to dart away and change its target to the line of Reapers.

"Avery, don't-," Shank pleaded as she began rushing forward.

But she was already a loose cannon. She charged at the demon, roaring with as much sound as she could possibly make. The beast crouched, giving pause as though confused as to what she was doing; it was then that she realized she wasn't so sure either. A revenant hurled a crate across the bison's face in the confusion, the demon rearing back with a roar before swiping its paw down at Avery.

She swung Hemlock before her just in time, the blade cutting through half of its paw to leave mangled claws on the cobblestone before her. The beast cried out in pain, eyes alight with fury and set on her as it lowered back down onto its three uninjured paws.

Moz had seized the opportunity, sliding beneath the belly of the beast to approach its head unseen. He thrust his blessed sword upwards, piercing the throat of the demon. It tried to cry out, black blood gurgling from the wound and splattering on Moz before he could roll out of the way.

The demon-bison buckled at the knees, hitting the cobblestone with a loud thud. All who were present watched with waiting eyes to see if the beast was truly gone. Avery looked from Moz as he wiped his face, to the splattered remains of the two men who weren't so lucky.

Moz took the hilt of his sword, still lodged in the leaking windpipe, and pulled it out with a sickening squish. He wiped away the black ooze from his blade with a black cloth before he crouched down to look at the mangled claws she had severed from the demon-bison, pinching the bridge of his nose between his thumb and pointer finger.

"It would seem that Paion's sword isn't so useless with demons after all," he said. "I wouldn't bet money or your life on being able to kill one. But this makes things admittedly easier."

Easier? Avery scowled. Two men were dead.

"Let's take them home. Wrap them in canvas... so their families don't have to see them," Avery said, catching Tristan nod before he went to retrieve the body bags.

She flinched at the loud snap of the match before lighting the tip of the incense cone. Waving out the flame of the match, she blew out the fire upon the tightly packed powder and a curl of smoke licked upwards towards the ceiling of the crimson chamber. She knelt at the altar held upon a stout table, hidden under a drape of silk the hue of blood. Though she had been told many times she had access to the royal family's private temple, the comfort of having a hearth shrine within her own bedroom was too appealing for her to have turned down.

Her spine was held straight and focused as she sat on folded knees and watched the smoke waver in a breeze that was not there. Without having to recall her years of disciplined devotion, she recited prayer.

"A child of the earth comes to honor the Gods. Bring unto my shrine the fires of wisdom. Bring unto my shrine the flow of the waters of life. Flow and flame and grow in me."

She reached out to close her fingers around the handle of the brass bell, ringing it thrice before bowing low to the ground. The silken black strands of her hair fell to the floor in front of her before she returned upright with closed eyes

"In the eyes of the Mothers who bore me, in the eyes of the Fathers who strengthened me, in the eyes of the Gods who guided me, make me one -"

The air in the chamber vibrated with a new presence, sending each hair on her arms and neck straight up. Her eyes flew open in alarm and she was momentarily disoriented by the sudden field of blood red that was the south wall of her royal chamber.

"*Princess, somebody is coming*!"

Her familiar's small voice warned her only seconds before the revenant was upon her. She stood, whirling in her robes to look behind her and she found herself startled not by his presence, but his young age. *Why, he's just a boy!*

His golden locks reflected the lanterns just as any breathing soul would have. He might have easily been mistaken for one of the living if it wasn't for the sour stench of the dead that rolled off his shoulders in waves; the boy must have travelled through Od to reach the castle. The dark golden eyes that watched her could have only foreshadowed dire news. She opened her mouth to speak, but he was faster.

"Princess Yumi, my name is Owen," he spoke in a voice that was both gentle and stern. "I have been sent to warn you of the Knights of Od that wish to take you into forced submission to the will of Beldam. They want the Knight of Spirit. I am also here to inform you that my mistress is coming this way to aid you. You may know her as the Berserker Witch."

"It's her!"

"What a strange name she has now!"

Yumi felt temporary relief when she saw the boy flinch at the choir of disembodied spirits; he heard them, too. It was short-lived, however, as her unease at the name sank in.

Whispers of the Berserker Witch reached every nook of Brightloch as quickly as the news of the massacre at Centralia flew in on the backs of carrier birds. Yumi looked to the fuzzy lop rabbit on the other side of the bed, but Mara said nothing.

"Your uncertainty is understood," Owen said, noticing her discomfort. "But if you'll allow me, I can show you the girl as we know her."

He held up his hands level with her forehead, hesitating to make contact. Yumi nodded.

"Do it," she murmured.

The icy hands touched her forehead, his thumbs across the front of her brow and his fingers reaching towards the back of her skull as though to carefully cradle her head. Silver fog clouded her vision as her sense of space gave way to Owen's memories.

She was standing in a graveyard embraced by iron gates with lush grass beneath her feet. Voices around her spoke mid-conversation, seemingly unaware of her presence.

"He will help you along the way, or until you've come to your senses."

Yumi turned to look at the man on her left. His presence was looming and tall, accentuated by his stovepipe hat and dark clothes. Yumi frowned. Who was he? This wasn't what the boy had been trying to show her.

She looked ahead and then understood. The young woman was looking straight at her, holding a rounded reading glass to her right eye as though to observe Yumi. She dropped the glass and it fell to her ribs, hanging on a brass necklace. It fell against an odd shirt, white and stained with blood. Bandages were wrapped around her waist and stained with the same rust red. What had happened to her?

"I can't hear what he's saying," she spoke and a tingling sensation crept from the base of her spine up the back of Yumi's neck. Her face was in full view as she frowned, blue eyes sliding from where Yumi stood seemingly undetected and towards the tall man.

The ground below Yumi's feet disappeared as the voices faded away, as the graveyard around them sank into darkness. She sat in emptiness, listening to the rise and fall of her own breath as she waited for whatever memory was to come next.

In the darkness, a bead of light began to grow and flicker in licks of orange. A warm glow that reflected off the trunks of trees told her she was in a forest. She was low to the ground; Owen had perhaps been sitting in this memory.

The girl was sitting with her bare knees pulled against her chest as though the campfire and leather jacket did not warm her enough. Yumi was close enough to see the light freckles on her cheeks and across the bridge of her nose that was wrinkled into a frown. Why? Where was she?

The dull mumble of men's voices came from somewhere nearby but Yumi understood nothing. She only watched the warm light on the face that she could not read as fearsome. Yumi yelped as she was yanked hard from that memory to another.

Rain poured down hard, soaking the clothes on everyone but Yumi. A large man and a companion with thick locks of hair were lifting someone with their shoulders; his face bloodied and unreadable. The sensation she felt was not chills, but the throaty growl of the beast within her reacting to what was unfolding before her. The Knight of Water.

She had been facing the Witch's back until she turned around. Her cheek was scraped and bleeding, the rain mixing the blood into a crimson watercolor on her flesh. Her wild waves of hair clung wet to her face as she looked at Yumi with serious eyes, much darker than even the memory she had just seen. What had happened between the two instances of time? Her green cloak was soaked, clinging to her arms and chest plate of brown leather.

"Owen," she commanded with eyes locked on Yumi. "Round up anyone hanging around this area. Go before us and see where the two snipers went."

Snipers? What is happening? Yumi opened her mouth and tried to plea for help, but no sound came as the world around her disappeared.

The final memory was the softest of them all. She was in a small house, dim but warm. The wood wall in front of her was littered with drawings, decorative arrows, maps, and horseshoes. Her line of vision turned towards windows of colorful glass, the sun shining through and bathing her in shades of turquoise and gold. The witch was standing before her, dry of any rain, and the scrape on her cheek was staunched. The colors reflected on her long waves of dark hair and Yumi noticed the cloak and armor were gone. Wherever they were standing was home to the Berserker Witch - she was somewhere safe.

"Can you do something for us?"

Her voice was soft and Yumi found herself wondering if the warm feeling belonged to her or to the ghost. She couldn't be sure.

"We found out that the last Knight is in Brightloch. Princess Yumi."

The chills returned when the witch spoke her name; Yumi hoped she would say it again.

"Is there any way you are able to go ahead of us and let her know we're coming? That we'll take her to safety before Morgana reaches her?"

Yumi lifted her hand, wanting to touch her unscathed cheek. The witch was coming to save her.

The world was swallowed in fog and Yumi grasped at empty air, desperate to anchor herself on the young woman to keep her from disappearing. She found herself back in her chamber as Owen was pulling his hands back. Her brow was heavy with sadness and the expression of bewilderment on Owen's face must have meant it was obvious.

"She's... coming here?"

Owen nodded. "Avery and the others made it a priority."

Warmth bloomed in her. *Avery*. Her name was Avery.

— 🕊 —

"So, what exactly was it that you were trying to accomplish by screaming at the demon like a madwoman?"

The question came from Shank as they left Centralia behind, but Moz was the one who laughed. Avery shrugged, trying to ignore the fact that his laugh had caught her off guard.

"Startle it? See if it would call me out on my bluff? I'm not actually sure, I didn't know what to do. The spirits refused to approach it."

"Let's not give that another try, alright? We got lucky this time, but we can't count on the surprise every time," Moz said, Avery almost missing the brief smile when she turned in his direction.

"Your ghosts were a bust," Alice cut in with a slight pout curled on her bottom lip. "We're going to have to find an altar to Onja or Moz has to do everything for every demon we encounter from here on out. And Brightloch is crawling with the bitches."

Avery frowned. Sure, the spirits wouldn't attack directly, but there was no doubt that their persistence in throwing whatever wasn't nailed to the ground helped their efforts.

"I reckon we might come upon a smaller village," Tristan stated. "One not on the maps. Or better yet, we come across a stray shrine. The forest between here an' Brightloch is littered with 'em so keep yer eyes peeled."

"Would you know what to do if we come across one?"

He nodded, looking down at Maria with a proud beam when he answered her.

"Course I do! Don't worry about that part, just make sure yer looking out for 'em!"

Not long after they had left Centralia, Avery was in the forest again. She knew she should have been tired of walking in the forest, but Avery was smiling at the sound of her boots once again treading through the fern.

Aegis trotted next to her feet, occasionally slinking through the sliver of space between them as though he wished to specifically irritate her. She willed herself not to let him agitate her - it would be a long journey ahead of them if she did.

"You're a foolish woman, Avery Porter."

Maria was absently staring at Ina's tail as they marched west and she tried to shake away the boredom that was already setting in after one day of travel. She knew it was going to be a long walk if she couldn't keep her mind busy.

"Stop!" Moz suddenly shouted, lifting his sword in front of him.

Maria halted, almost tumbling over Ina. The black wolf stood still as stone at the head of the group, sniffing the air above their heads for any indication of what was ahead. Next to her, Avery had drawn out her sword and held her left palm near it; she was ready to slice open her palm to call upon her revenant army.

"There's a Knight ahead. I think it's Peter," Moz finally said.

Avery looked at him in bewilderment. "But not Morgana?"

He only shook his head before holding a finger up to his lips, signaling for the rest of the group to hush. Moz spun around until he was facing Maria and looked down at Ina. There was a long pause before the large wolf cautiously padded into the trees. Maria had almost forgotten that he could talk to the demons in their heads now; or at least he didn't have to pretend that he couldn't hear them. She wasn't exactly certain of the specifics just yet.

They waited in a gaping silence that made room for the rolls of thunder miles away and the late summer humidity hung heavy in the air. Moz stared into the trees, watching Ina cautiously creep forward. The demon companion paused before running back to them quicker than she had left. Shank was the first to react.

"A whole group? How many do you think?"

Ina huffed through her snout and Moz was next to translate. "Ten. Maybe more waiting at a distance to see what we do."

"We might have an edge if we attack first," Avery said as she looked to Kurosaki and Moz for confirmation before taking a headcount. "Five... six... seven against ten isn't awful odds, and with the element of surprise..."

Maria looked to Moz. He was pinching the bridge of his nose with his head down in his signature sign of frustration.

"Avery's right. We need to clear them out of our path to Brightloch. The sooner, the better. Lead the way, Ina."

Ina trotted ahead of the group, ducking her head low to pick up any scent that the Beldam's Legion might have laid on the earth.

They walked at a hurried pace for what felt like an hour before Ina froze, her ears perking upwards and she crouched low on her haunches as though to lay low against the bed of moss. A faint murmur of voices began echoing off the trees. Maria and the others stood in the middle of a clearing they had only half-crossed. Had they fallen into a trap? They were entirely exposed!

Maria pulled her arrow back when she saw the mass of charcoal uniforms appear from the trees - of mostly uniforms, anyway. A figure stood apart from the gray mass in a light cotton shirt and riding pants, seeming to be a young woman. Maria swore out loud, did the Legion have a new alliance somewhere? With the Reapers from Eyon? From where she stood behind the line of swords, she saw Moz suddenly flinch.

"Avery, don't!"

It was too late. Avery abandoned her position, holding Hemlock with only one hand as she ran toward the embrace of the enemy.

"LILY!" She shrieked.

Maria saw the young woman lurch into action, running towards them as she called Avery's name in mirrored desperation. Moz sprinted from his post as well, chasing after Avery to either drag her back or protect her as the members of the Legion readied themselves for

Avery's sword. Maria stepped forward to fill the empty spot beside Tristan that Moz had abandoned. Her stance was ready to fire if her friends were threatened and surely she wouldn't drop out like Moz just had - *that idiot.*

"What the hell is going on?"

"I might be wrong, but I reckon that's the girl from Avery's apartment in Ardua. She almost ruined this whole thing, what is she doing here?"

The young woman tried throwing her arms around Avery in a tight embrace as they met, but Avery grabbed her by the arm, pulling the woman backwards before throwing her into the direction of their group and sent the young woman stumbling towards Maria.

"Don't let Lily watch!"

Maria was startled by Avery's sudden demand and she looked at the woman, who was watching Avery run back in the direction of the enemy. Sweat glinted off Lily's umber cheekbones as she watched with gaping confusion, her bow idle at her side. *What the fuck does she want me to do?*

"If you go behind the trees, we'll—" Maria started.

The woman shot her a sharp look, pointedly not backing down from Maria. "Don't you dare tell me what to do."

Charming. Maria shrugged; she tried. She turned her attention back forward with her arrow pulled back, ready to launch it as soon as Avery or Moz were threatened. The ribbon of blood twirling around Avery's open palm sent chills down Maria's neck as the air went cold with the breath of the dead. Even Aegis' fur stood on end as his Mistress' eyes glazed over with the white fog of death and the long tendrils of her dark hair lifted. Black shadows crawled upwards from the underworld, slipping through the dirt with ease.

Maria couldn't help but slide her gaze towards the woman, now watching with her mouth agape in astonishment.

"It's... it's her," the woman whispered, her horror just loud enough for Maria to hear.

"The Berserker Witch!" a member of the Legion cried out from the opposing mass of swords before they broke apart to rush Avery and Moz.

Avery threw her bleeding hand forward and the revenants led the assault. With the ghostly front line in place, Tristan, Kurosaki, and Alice jumped into the fray with their swords.

Maria sidestepped until her angle allowed her to launch arrows into the flesh of enemies who hesitated - probably wondering if it would be better to face the Knight of Od or the necromancer. She had expected the ghosts to slash at their skin with only moderate injury, but a melody of cracking bones met with the clang of Moz's sword. But how? Why was Avery's attack getting gradually stronger?

Maria maneuvered towards Moz, knowing that the ghosts weren't as protective of him as they were of Avery. She tried not to become distracted by his violent dance - the waltz of his feet always finding the right place to be and his blessed sword becoming increasingly faster than the one it clashed with. And when the moment was right, she knew the grin that would spread upon his face before a nebula of blood tainted his opponent and the dance came to a ghastly end.

Maria didn't realize she was hypnotized until the large body was upon her; an officer of the Beldam's Legion had somehow slipped in from the periphery the battle. She hollered for help; she knew she would be unable to finish drawing her arrow before he would strike her down.

There was no time to form the words before an arrow became lodged in his eye socket. Blood and other unsightly fluids spurted from the wound as the man sank to his knees and fell forward on a mangled face, the arrow punched through soft skin before snapping in half under his dead weight.

Maria whipped around, ready to look at Shank in amazement at their accuracy when she saw the empty bow in Lily's hands

"Damn," Maria whispered low enough for no one else to hear but nodded her head once in thanks. The look she got in return screamed *turn the fuck around!*

"Where is Morgana hiding!" Moz hollered to no specific Legion member before cutting down the man in front of him. He received no answer and Maria launched arrows at the enemy before he carried on in gruesome fury.

Maria caught a flash of spectacles and she whirled to locate Peter, her heart racing when she found him trudging through his comrades towards Moz. When she set her sights on his shaved head, her face scrunched in fury and she shot arrows in his direction.

They hurtled close to their mark but did not land. Peter turned towards her from across the fray with a devilish smirk.

"Oh fuck," Maria said breathlessly, remembering Moz pulling Kurosaki's bullet out of his forehead. The arrow couldn't harm Peter even if it did hit its mark.

"Moz!"

No sooner than when Maria called out his name to warn him, she saw Moz turn his head towards the other Knight and his mouth curling in an ugly scowl. Maria edged even closer as Moz stomped towards Peter, quickly cutting down a Legion member who tried to stop him. Peter's eyes flickered to the staccato sounds of snapping bones as Avery picked off his subordinates one by one; was that a flash of fear she saw across his face?

Metal clashed as their swords met, Peter reacted just as fast to Moz's rapid hits. Peter was Moz's equal in the deadly dance.

"This isn't how it's supposed to go," she heard Peter call out. "I could fight with you all day, William.

But when you die, you will die at the hands of your brothers and sisters as the things we truly are."

With its target in a stationary position, Shank's arrow pierced Peter's left cheek. Peter slipped out of Moz's swinging range and ripped the arrow out with a cry of pain, tossing the arrow to the ground and crushing it under his boot. The Knight's cheek leaked far less blood than Maria would have expected from any ordinary person.

"But I will give you one more chance to be on the right side of history," Peter continued, unfazed as the flapping flesh of his cheek was already beginning to seal itself with new skin. "Helping us will create balance between the gods and Beldam."

Maria's eyes widened at the superhuman healing - that must have been how Moz healed his shoulder wounds so quickly. *Damn, why couldn't Balthazar make my healing hands that fast?*

Moz's sword slashed at Peter's waist with an angry thrust before he stepped backwards.

"Is that what she told you? You'll believe anything, Pete."

Peter grimaced, quickly scanning his gaze around the stained meadow to see the sparse number of his allies still alive. Surely the Knight would continue even after he was the last one standing, Maria couldn't see why not.

She was proven wrong as he shrunk backwards in a gesture that appeared to be cowardice at face-value. Peter wished to utterly destroy Moz but chose instead to protect the lives of his surviving troops.

Why care if your men died if you were going to tear down the veil between the living and dead?

"Firm in your foolish beliefs," Peter spat. "Men, retreat!"

Her eyes widened and Maria tried to hit as many targets as she could before they disappeared into the trees, the ordinary Reapers fleeing before their Knight did. Arrows were lodged in a few shoulders as she hit a few of her targets, but she certainly would not be getting them back.

With a howl of rage, Moz made a final drive at Peter and his sleek sword pierced Peter's stomach. Peter let out a gurgling laugh as though the attack didn't even surprise him and with a jerky movement, he wedged himself off the blade.

"You'll get that battle you so desperately wanted; you can't protect the Knight of Spirit forever. We're coming for you and we're coming for the witch."

Peter's eyes glazed over black behind his glasses and in a violent blur of upward motion, he vanished.

They stood unopposed in the field, their shoulders bobbing as they all tried to catch their breath and slow their racing hearts. Moz was the one who voiced their frustrations regarding the rather unimportant bodies they had cut down.

"She sends in her pawns to die and doesn't even show her face? Morgana, you cowardly bitch."

He let out an unintelligible yell, the sheer release of volume seeming to help soothe his rage before he turned around to regroup with the rest of the dissenting Reapers.

Avery lowered her sword, her chest heaving as she tried to catch her breath. She stood for a tense moment just staring at them. Her hair fell to her back and her eyes returned to steel blue. Maria sympathized with the pang of shame on her face, the same one that was on hers long ago in Wrencrest. When she had stared at

Firefly unable to find the words to explain her fall to Mona's witchcraft.

Avery used the corner of her cloak to wipe the splatters of blood from her face and slowly stepped forward. Moz rejoined them first, sheathing his sword before shrinking away from Lily and Maria.

"Give them space," he hissed through his teeth, but none of them listened. Maria's feet felt rooted into the ground as though the fear that Avery was certainly feeling was her own.

Avery finally crumpled into a heap at Lily's feet. The heavy sobs Avery unleashed were clearly held inside her for a very long time and the sound pierced Maria to the core. Lily was turning her confused, gaping mouth in the direction of everyone in the circle as she looked for an explanation. Maria looked at Moz, expecting him to say something first. His eyes were only wide with shock as though Avery's sudden wails somehow broke something fundamental inside of him.

Aegis was the first to act, crawling into Avery's lap and disappearing behind her curtain of dark hair. Though Maria only heard mewing, she tried to pretend he was saying something at least remotely comforting.

Lily finally put her bow down on the ground and bent down to meet her friend. Though she said nothing, she waited in quiet patience with both of her hands on each small shoulder.

"Please.... Let me, give me the chance... to explain everything," Avery sobbed.

— 🕊 —

"Does it alarm you?"

Morgana crossed her legs, the height of the limb she sat upon as she watched the fray did not make her at all nervous. But she knew that's not what the Knight meant.

"He's not giving way," she replied.

Peter, who was standing next to her, looked down as she spoke. As someone who also harbored a Knight of Od, he knew exactly whom she was speaking to. Where she ruled the fire, he ruled the air; the swirling winds and dragons etched into his left arm made it clear to anyone who saw Peter. Strong and solemn mountains adorned her daughter, Sera, on the right leg. Morgana had only seen a glimpse of the tumultuous sea on the right arm of William

Mosley. Whoever was the Knight of Spirit would be marked in such a way to connect all their limbs, uniting the Knights in a way easily concealed.

"If you don't give the Beldam what She wants, you won't ever see your husband again. Our young William has bested you at every meet and yet you are so calm. Why?"

"Because I know that deep down, you are Her creations. He can only fight against the hunger for destruction for so long. With each death he is responsible for, another seed is planted for the desire to tear down the veil between the living and the dead."

There was a silence; the Knight was done talking. Peter glanced down at her, as though waiting to see if he had the opportunity now to speak.

"The Berserker Witch happens to be the same person that Miss Lily Clements was searching for," he stated. "We pulled out when Mosley refused to let the Knight engage. He saw no need to risk becoming vulnerable. Undoubtedly, it would serve us far better to let them lead us to the Knight of Spirit."

Morgana let herself slip from the tree limb, falling the great distance to the ground with her cloak flapping wildly behind her. The earth crunched under the hard impact of her boots, she bobbed with her bent knees and stood back upright as though she had only jumped mere feet. She turned around and looked up at Peter, expecting her brother in Knighthood to follow.

"Nothing has changed, o' Knight of Air. All this has done was make our predicament slightly more interesting. I still have every intention of killing the witch for what she has done to my own flesh and blood. She dies after we have Mosley. Slow agony, by my own hands."

Her insides boiled with anger with the memory of finding Sera limping towards the crew, the fear that sparked wildly in her eyes; the same eyes that belonged to Sera's father. Peter jumped the distance much faster than she had, his cooperation with the Knight allowing him to move effortlessly through the air.

"Then we will save her for you," he offered. "Do it with your bare hands."

Morgana looked over her shoulder at him with a satisfied smirk. "I knew there was a reason you were my favorite Brother."

CHAPTER FOUR

TEMPERANCE

They had walked for miles with their weapons at the ready for the rest of the Legion members who were certainly waiting for them. Maria waited for their vengeance, but sundown came first.

A tense silence clung to them the entire way as they waited for Avery to speak first, but her dry expression of panic held - her blue eyes widened, even her freckles paled - until they had decided to make camp for the night.

Yards away from the crackling fire, Avery began to explain Reaperdom and their current situation to Lily; Maria helped to fill in the in holes when Avery couldn't find the right words.

As Maria sat with them, her mind began drifting off and the words became a dull mumble around her. Their words weren't necessarily boring to her; she just couldn't help but watch Moz as he was watching them. He stood at the base of a large oak away from where Shank, Tristan, Alice, and Kurosaki had been talking at the fireside. As he stood in isolation as he watched Maria. She followed his line of sight without turning her head. No, he watched Avery.

Suddenly everything made sense. His reaction to Avery's weepy confession to Lily. The way he treated her ever since the time the Knight first broke out. He was kinder, warmer, and once again the Moz that Maria once knew him to be.

Still, she had to know for sure. Maria stood up and walked towards the others, off to the side of Moz's line of vision as he continued to watch Avery and Lily.

"You're in love," Maria blurted out as she approached Moz at the tree.

"Maria, I thought we agreed on leaving it in the ground. I don't feel that way about you anymore."

She couldn't help but laugh at his quick deflection, as though he had been anticipated her bringing it up and rehearsed the dismissal. The sound was biting and sarcastic, but well-deserved in her opinion.

"Bah! Don't be such an idiot!"

He began walking deeper into the forest, but she knew that Moz could not dodge her that easily.

"You're upset. You know now that she's reunited with her friend, she's going to leave and you'll never see her again," she said. Moz stopped with his back still to Maria. He said nothing, only looking halfway over his shoulder before disappearing into the trees.

She rolled her eyes. "What a drama queen."

Maria returned to where she had left Avery and Lily just as they were standing up from where they had planted themselves for the undoubtedly difficult conversation.

"How am I supposed to explain what I just saw otherwise," she caught Lily saying. "I mean, as much as I'd love reason right now... there just isn't any. And I hate to admit it but the more I think about it, the more is explained. You changed so suddenly."

"What do you mean?" Avery was wiping wet streaks off her own cheeks when Maria approached with her canteen held up in offer. She accepted, gulping down water while Lily answered.

"Well, before you broke up with Riko I could hardly get you to stay inside. You were gone all the time and living your life; nothing on this earth could have stopped you from going where you wanted. And then suddenly you barely left our apartment. You used to talk to strangers like they were your friends and then you shut out anyone that wasn't me. Even Byron noticed the change in you and I couldn't figure out why you would do that to your own brother. But me? I may have lost you if I wasn't with you every day.

The depression was incredibly obvious… if, you know, Reaping was what you were doing when you finally did go out, well... I can see why. But never in my wildest dreams would I have guessed that the myths were true."

Maria wondered if any of her friends in Wrencrest had noticed a change in her when she became a Reaper. If Firefly did, she didn't say anything; she would have been the closest to notice, aside from Shank. A pale flicker caught her attention from the periphery of her vision and Maria forced out the name with a mental shove.

"Avery, you're very lucky to have someone so close to you see a thing like that," Maria said, trying to ignore the phantom that made itself known at every mere thought of Firefly's name. She knew there would never come a day where the whisper of her name didn't summon her image; not after what Maria did to her. What would have happened if the girl had simply died, no questions asked?

Maria watched Lily straighten her back with her hands on her knees, looking out into the trees. Her dark eyes were wide, as though keeping them open might help her absorb the fantastic information.

"This really doesn't leave room for disbelief about any of the other myths, does it," Lily finally said jokingly after a moment of silence, looking from Avery to Maria. Her expression then changed from stunned to sheer wonder and Maria felt her cheeks grow warm as though she was being analyzed as some mystical creature. She hardly wanted to point out the inevitable disappointment.

"If it's any consolation, we can't actually appear out of thin air or know your darkest secret," Maria offered and Lily laughed. She turned away sheepishly, not understanding why her face was suddenly feeling so much warmer.

– ❦ –

"I reckon we should have Moz come back," Tristan said, looking up from the pile of branches he was assembling into a campfire. Because she was the closest, the expectant look fell on Avery and she nodded.

"I'll go get him," she offered, strapping Hemlock onto her back as a precautionary measure; she was not entirely convinced yet that the Legion was not still lurking amongst the tree trunks.

Maria looked over her shoulder at her with a flicker of what Avery could have sworn was excitement before it quickly disappeared. She lifted a finger and pointed in the direction past where Kurosaki stood.

"He went that way, certainly not that far."

"Thanks," Avery said with a nod before she began walking.

The deeper into the woods she walked, the cooler and sweeter the air became. Avery stopped, inhaling the feeling the forest gave her and exhaling the tension she realized she had still kept locked in her muscles. She stepped carefully over a fallen tree and turned her feet slightly sideways to move down the hill towards where she saw Moz's tall frame on the edge of her vision with his back to her; *what is he doing?*

"Do you need an escort back to Ardua?"

His voice was flat as Avery approached. Though his back was to her, she knew the Knight in Moz had alerted him of her presence.

"No, why would I?" Avery leaned back against the tree closest to her.

"Because you found Lily, just like you promised her. You don't need us; this was never your fight."

"Why am I under the impression that this is distressing to you? I thought you were eager for me to leave," she spoke with a sharper voice, caught off guard by his words. "It wasn't at first, but it's my fight now."

What is he getting at? Did Moz believe that she would abandon everything when she got what she wanted? It was insulting, at best. He was the one originally adamant against her being there in the first place.

"Why was I under the impression that you weren't here because you felt captive, but that you wanted to be?"

He turned around with a face painted in both hurt and anger.

"Because it's true! Moz, don't forget that I was your captive and you said cruel things! And still even now, here I am," her voice shook even harder when she tried not to let it. Avery willed herself not to cry but failed.

She could see the guilt in his face and Moz stepped forward to close the distance. He cupped the side of her cheek with his hand, his palms rough and worn but held a comforting warmth. Her face flushed hot when she felt the tear on her cheek dribble onto his fingers. He was touching her - why?

"I was awful when I tried to hide the Knight and I failed so terribly. You didn't deserve any of the terrible things I said and did. I'm trying to make up for that, all the time."

Avery stood still in silent shock at his touch and couldn't form words when she realized that it was still there. Her fingers scratched against the bark of the tree behind her, not sure what a proper response would be to such a gentle statement. She searched his face for any signs of his characteristic rage, for any signs of the person who held her at knifepoint not that long ago. It was not in the few freckles on his nose, not in the edges of his jaw. Nor was it in the white of his scar or the moss in his eyes. He had softened for this moment.

A woozy feeling washed over her; why was his face so close to hers? She opened her mouth to speak but trailed off when he slowly dipped his head down. There was a pause as though he waited for her to yell and push him away, but she did not.

The kiss was tender and light as air, as though Moz thought she may shatter under the most delicate touch. His fingers slid backward across her cheek and swam in her hair. Tendrils of his hair brushed against her nose, sending a wave of electricity through her nerves and she did everything she could to get him closer. Her fingers closed around his shoulder, the other on his forearm. Any tenderness gave way to desperation for contact and Avery gripped a little tighter.

And then it was over. He looked down at her with wide eyes, perhaps in disbelief at what he had just done. She knew the same look was smeared on her own face.

"Moz," she whispered his name, not sure what else to say. His face was still so close; she was about to stand on her toes to close the distance and send their lips crashing together again when he stepped backwards out of her grip.

"I never meant for that to happen," he murmured.

Her expression fell and the warm high she felt faded instantly. She had no words, so she stood feeling like an idiot with her mouth hanging slightly open as though the wind she caught in her teeth might make the words for her. If he never meant for that to happen, then why did it?

Moz sank into the shadows, leaving Avery alone.

Still she stood in shock, unable to determine if the kiss had really happened or if it was some vivid dream that took her by surprise. Why would she even dream up such a thing? She touched her bottom lip with two fingers and found she was still buzzing with warm static.

And he regretted it; certainly the ecstatic feeling she had was supposed to be regretted as well. Avery turned around and inhaled deeply with a lift of her shoulders.

"Then I will pretend nothing ever happened," she said to herself and the trees as her only witnesses. Avery turned and trudged back up the hill to the campfire; her legs felt much heavier going up alone than they did walking to Moz.

Upon her return, she found that her friends were just as she left them; Moz sitting amongst them as though he had never left. Avery knew better when he didn't look up at her. Her heart pounded with the realization of the interaction, or lack thereof.

She crossed the group to find that Lily had been standing, swaying on her heels with the waves of leaves in the wind - Lily Clements never needed the excuse of music to find herself dancing.

Avery smiled but tried to step past her to take a seat. Lily's fingers closed around her elbow and yanked Avery back in her direction. She snickered, agreeing to twirl once under Lily's poised hand.

"Why so stern? You don't have work tomorrow, you don't have anywhere you need to be at this moment," Lily said, both Avery's hands in hers and swaying her like a marionette.

Avery then surrendered, her motions made by her own volition as they danced to the music made only by the snapping of the fire and rolling howl of the wind over the treetops. She knew it was there with Lily that the life she had loved before escaping Ardua could meet with the wilderness she found growing and thriving in her.

— ❧ —

Moz had seen the brightness of love in her face as she danced around the campfire with the friend that meant the world to her. The same love was there when Ina nuzzled her immediately upon meeting and when she stopped to look in wonder at the nature he had thought they were simply passing through. There was love in the forgiveness she offered even when he didn't deserve it. Avery was not short of love; in fact, she was spilling over with it.

It could not have been her missing emotion. She could not ever become a mere repeat of his mistake with Maria.

The worst part of it all? He couldn't even touch it. Couldn't hold a candle to it. Once he had realized that the desire was his own, and not that of the Knight, he knew he had to keep her away from the monstrosity that lurked within him. As long as there was a Knight of Water, he could not come near Avery in that way again. Luckily for them both, she seemed fine - even after his awful blunder.

Moz fumbled with a hand in his pocket, fishing for his rolled tobacco and matches. He struck the match with a snap and lit the roll as he held it between his teeth, the scent of clove curling around his nostrils. He felt the Knight stirring, shrinking backwards into the farthest corners of him to get away. If he couldn't rid himself of it completely, he could smoke the fucker out as best he could.

When he looked up, he caught the familiarly suspicious curve of Maria's brows. He was thankful when Tristan spoke, taking her attention off him as Lily and Avery sat back down with grinning faces.

"So y'knew Avery before she was a Reaper then?"

Lily nodded in response, her braids bobbing. "Since we were children, my family adopted her when she was sixteen. Well, I guess I was the only one who was a child."

Avery flinched as though the comment stung her, but Moz found she smiled upon her friend as though in immediate forgiveness. Unconditional love surfaced again.

"What was she like," Shank asked with their focus down on the bird they were peeling off the spit, hissing with a shaking hand before putting their burned thumb into their mouth.

Moz watched as Lily turned to look at Avery, Avery's eyes wide and she was ready to drink in everything Lily had to say as though she didn't know the answer herself. Lily's smile held what could have been fondness or sadness - he wasn't quite sure.

"Avery loved her parents with all of her heart– Katherine and Harrison Porter. Avery was their whole world and she was the very model of filial piety as a kid," she said.

Avery was watching her with tears in her eyes, drinking in Lily's every word. "My parents," she echoed with soft sadness.

Why the sadness? Moz wondered if perhaps Mr. and Mrs. Porter had passed away as his own parents did centuries ago. He thought that would have explained the adoption, but Lily did not touch the subject again.

"Avery was a cellist, but only because I convinced her to try it. Ironically, she stuck with music instead of me. She never played after when I think she was a

Reaper. She skated, and though I know nothing about it, it seemed like she was pretty damn good. Um, what else..."

Lily furrowed her brows and pursed her lips in thought. "I don't know what else you want me to say. She couldn't cook for shit. She had a long-time girlfriend she loved very much, up until being a Reaper, I guess."

"Girlfriend?" Alice asked, her eyebrow raised in piqued interest.

Avery nodded. "Ex. I'm bisexual."

"Avery broke up with her not too long before you took her. Riko was-" Lily tried to keep talking until Kurosaki cut her off abruptly.

Kurosaki suddenly stood up. "Riko? Riko who?"

Moz followed everyone else's look towards Kurosaki, his slender face twisted in what could have been concern or anger.

"Riko Yamada. Why?"

Kurosaki rubbed his hand down his face once and stepped away with his back to them, his other hand on his hip. Moz stood up, alarmed by his reaction.

"Izaya, what's going on?"

He looked from Kurosaki to Alice, who was still sitting but held her head between both hands with a gaping look of shock in her amber eyes that seemed to be absently focused on a point somewhere in the flames in front of her. When Kurosaki finally turned around, he locked eyes with Avery.

"I need to talk with you in private."

She stood up, clutching her arms with a look of fright. "Can I... please, can Lily come, too?"

"Whatever you want," Kurosaki said and strode past them to lead Avery and Lily away, out of earshot.

Moz looked to Alice; she seemed to have an idea of what was going on and why Kurosaki had reacted to the name the way he did.

"Care to explain?"

Without moving her head, her golden eyes looked up at him.

"Riko Yamada is the name of a Soul Harvester in Ardua."

As Kurosaki led her and Lily away, Avery tried not to let the panic show in her voice.

"W-what's going on?"

He stopped when they were yards away from the campfire and safely out of earshot. Kurosaki's look was grave and Avery felt her stomach drop as he struck a match.

"I need you to roll up your sleeves. Both of them."

She did as she was told, the sleeves of both her arms rolled up to her elbow.

"Farther," he instructed.

Avery frowned as she struggled to roll them up higher, the fabric becoming increasingly difficult to fold until she was able to push them half-way up her biceps. Kurosaki took hold of her left wrist, fingers closed around her blood bracelet. She watched in confusion as he examined the inside of her elbow, his match held closely for light.

"You never questioned what these marks were?"

"What are you talking about?"

She had never noticed them until they were pointed out. Avery bent her head to look at what he was talking about and in the dim light managed to see them: faint pocks of darker skin in the inside of her elbow, suspiciously close to where the blue of her veins snaked through her arm.

Kurosaki dropped her arm gently and looked at her with sincere sadness - the most honest display of emotion Avery had seen from Kurosaki in the short time she had known him.

"I knew Riko Yamada," he said softly. "Though she's a human, she's gotten herself horribly intertwined with Reapers. Not to lessen the severity of this or shift the blame onto you, but she is a member of Morgana's police department and her vileness could have been predicted."

The beating in Avery's chest froze and she felt the heavy silence that the absence of his words left. Riko Yamada, the detective of the Ardua Police Department. Why did she fail to draw the connection? She had assumed that maybe, just maybe, there were at least some employees doing the job they had appeared to be there for.

"Yamada was my travelling companion," he continued. "Until one day in Centralia she made an attempt on my life, claiming a wolf spoke to her. Riko believed she could become immortal if she killed a Reaper to absorb their power. In hindsight, that wolf was definitely Sera's familiar - she was trying to kill us off to get to Moz."

"Needless to say, I didn't stick around after that. Other Reapers we know found that Ardua had a system of lures for soul harvesting, usually located in gentlemen's clubs or bars. Crippled souls would be attracted and demons would latch on... Avery, Riko had a hand in one of these places. I don't want to jump to conclusions.... but it sure looks like she was using you as bait to lure vulnerable people into these places."

By the time he had stopped talking, she was staring blankly at the ground with wet cheeks. The sneering grins of the men who called out to her, the very night she was attacked by the Leeches. Did they know her by name? *Gods, what have they done to me?*

Avery's stomach lurched at the thought and found an itch in the base of her throat that made her want to vomit, but she was left dry as bleached bone. The sickening feeling of being so horribly violated - even as an empty, soulless vessel - made her want to crawl out of her own skin.

"I don't know what Morgana promised her in exchange for making demons," he said softly. "But make no mistake, Riko got something out of it. I know nothing can change what I speculate happened, but I'm sorry. I'm really fucking sorry, Avery."

From behind her, Lily whirled Avery around and pulled her into a hug. Her hand held Avery's head against the base of her throat, shielding her from the outside world as Lily remained frozen in shock.

"None of what you told us leaves this conversation, understand?"

"I do," Kurosaki answered Lily's sharp order of protection. "Though Alice already gathered what I did. She knows about Riko as well."

The sunny smile, the faint freckles, the wise eyes. All belonging to an incarnation of evil that she had unsuspectingly kissed and called "dear". She was used the entire time. How many other hands had laid themselves upon her with sinister intentions? She felt their phantom fingers skimming across her flesh and knotting in her hair across her scalp and she was overwhelmed with a wish for death.

Avery shut down. Only faintly aware of the sound of the wind and Lily's hand in her hair, nothing else passed through her brain. She had almost missed Kurosaki's words when he spoke with a dark tone, his strikingly dark eyebrows furrowing over his eyes and casting a daunting shadow on his gaunt face.

"I've already set myself on killing Riko. But I think you have a much bigger stake in this. Avery, when the time comes, you'll be the one to make her pay."

Her lungs clenched in her ribs, the world around her growing smaller and smaller as her heart pounded. Avery took shallow and staggered breaths, trying to stay afloat in a sea that wasn't there. Her vision rattled and she felt herself slip out of her body, detached from the person named Avery Porter. Dying, she was going to die. Right there in the arms of her friend.

She heard their voices but couldn't process the words. She was only vaguely aware of her own movement as she was lowered to the ground in a sitting position, her gaze fixed on her knees.

"-he knows what to do when this happens, Maria has panic attacks," Kurosaki's voice faded. She *was* dying. She sat in darkness for an eternity until a new voice came from somewhere in front of her.

"Can you hear me, Avery?"

She didn't answer Moz, she only thought it was Moz; voices were warped and drowned out by the sensation of her pulse pounding in her ears.

"I'm gonna touch your feet, alright? And I want you to nod your head when you can feel it."

Still she made no attempt to answer what she thought he had said. Avery felt gentle pressure pushing through both boots, pressing onto her toes.

"Can you feel that?"

She swayed gently where she sat, too disoriented to answer.

"Avery, please tell me if you can feel that," he repeated firmly.

She nodded, not bothering to form an answer for him verbally as the pressure of what might have been his thumbs kept fast on her feet.

"Good, now inhale deeply through your nose and exhale through your mouth."

Moz's voice somehow had become so soothing and the waters of fear around her felt smoothed by his gentle words. She did as she was told, her shoulders shaking as she took in all the air she could - it felt cold and deadly within her lungs. She exhaled quickly, eager to push it out.

"Alright Avery, we'll take it slow next time. Can you feel my fingers on your knees?"

The thumbs pressed gently into her bent kneecaps, making Avery aware of the distance between her toes and her knees. She slowly remembered the presence of her legs, the way she was connected to the ground. Her head bobbed slowly.

"Good. Now inhale through your nose again and exhale through your mouth."

He gently pinched Avery's hand between his pointer fingers and thumbs, asking her again if she could feel the sensation. She could feel not only the pressure, but felt strange static through her nerves when Moz touched her skin again. When she nodded, he asked her to wiggle her fingers in addition to breathing.

She focused hard on the tendons in her fingers, willing them to wag and found herself pleased when they obeyed.

"Good," he spoke again and moved his hands to hold the sides of her head gently. "Are you aware of your head in relationship to the rest of your body? How it tells you to move?"

Avery knew she should have been embarrassed, but she simply felt too exhausted. She nodded once as much as her body would allow her to, the appeal of laying flat on the ground making her sink slightly to her side.

"You're safe right now, we're all safe, and we're all going to fix this together. Lily loves you and we all love you. Nothing that Riko did to you changes the person you are now," he said before letting go of her.

Avery swayed sleepily before she felt Lily's hand close around her arm. "C'mon, let me help you up."

She clumsily rose to her feet with Lily's help and was slowly guided back over to the campfire. Avery was met with silence from everyone else - did they know, too? She was too tired to care, too tired to look up from her shoes to find any indication in their faces. She wasn't, however, too tired to recognize that this was quite possibly the worst day of her life.

Aegis approached her, not speaking to her and instead rubbed himself against her boot. She sank to the ground with her legs folded, scooping him into her arms.

For just a moment, she wanted to coddle an ordinary house cat.

"I can't help but feel as though I'm also to blame, Avery. I was in this body for a whole week before your Inception and I noticed nothing. I'm sorry."

She fell slowly to her side, letting her bones sink into the dirt as she let go of her exhaustion.

"I forgive you," she whispered to the cat, letting him slink out of her arms.

She slipped into a slumber of wordless dreams and constantly morphing faces, unsure that she remembered what her parents had looked like and what their voices had sounded like to the ears of her empty shell - an imposter of the child they had wanted so desperately to love.

— 🐦 —

Moz sank to the ground, his knees folding under him to sit alone where Lily and Avery had left him–close enough to still see the fire but too far to feel its warmth. He had watched Aegis slink out from the crumpled heap that was a sleeping Avery and sit himself before Mori; he had tuned them out when he realized they were talking about Riko Yamada. It wasn't his business.

Instead of partaking in the information spreading, which was on the verge of becoming cruel gossip, Ina walked quietly towards Moz. She made it halfway between him and the rest of the group before he shook his head.

"I want to be alone."

"You and I know that's not true. What happened to honesty, William?"

The black wolf was the only one of them who had insisted on calling him by his first name no matter how much he protested. This time he didn't argue at his name nor at the fact that she had sat herself down right next to him anyway.

"Maria's right, you know."

Moz scowled; nosy animal.

"You can't deny anything if you're making that face, child. You're allowed to be in love."

"Did you just trot over here to chastise me? That base has already been covered and I hardly think now is the appropriate time," he snapped defensively.

"You've already kissed her, it's the only thing running through your mind right now. What are you running from? Or better yet - what do you think you're saving her from?"

He thought the answer would have been plain as day: the Knight. The reason he had left her there was the Knight, he was beginning to get too close and he couldn't allow that.

"Admit it to me, right now. Get it off your chest so that you can do what you foolishly believe you must."

"The only foolish belief would be that I'm entitled to feel this way even when I know the consequences and dangers," he growled back. "The only option is to put what I have just done behind us and keep doing what I must as a friend."

Ina sat up, circling around him once before stopping to face him. Jack emerged from the pocket of his coat, nose twitching as he peeked to see what was going on. If he had been speaking, Moz couldn't hear him with his conversation with Ina still engaged.

"You have your prerogatives as a man. But don't forget that time waits for no one."

As she walked back towards the bonfire, Moz looked down at the tiny face of his demon familiar. Jack looked back at him with happy, beady eyes.

"Don't worry, Master. Surely you know what is best!"

They held eye contact for a long moment before Moz picked up the rat and cradled him in his hands. The only kindness he would ever receive deservedly came from the small creature who knew both Moz and the Knight so well; they were equals.

"I don't think I do. Not this time."

"Somebody help!"

The crash and the cry of the little boy echoed off the cypress trees and bounced back up from the murky waters of the Wrencrest swamps. Chills ran up Maria's spine - she knew exactly what was happening.

Shank looked up from whatever device it was they had been assembling, she couldn't remember what they had called it. They jumped up from where they had sat down on the porch of the home perched in the trees, looking down and over the balcony ledge. Maria already knew what they would see; already knew this was a memory she couldn't yank herself out of.

"It's Cricket, something's happened!"

Shank dumped the pulleys and ropes onto the ground and ran for the wooden steps that wrapped around the trunk of the tree, their boots not taking long to start stomping on the pier planks below them. Croxi left his perch on the wood balcony, soaring downwards towards the swamp after Shank. Maria had not willed herself to move and yet she found herself teleported right behind her friend as they ran towards the terror-stricken child.

The little boy's face was bright red with tears as he pointed to the body floating in the water, both with the same pale hair. The figure's patterned skirts and brick red blouse were waterlogged as she floated just below the surface amongst the splintered boards. Shank looked above their heads at the house in the trees, the whole front half of it gone and floating in the swamp. They jumped into the waters, vanishing into the murkiness before bobbing back up. Maria watched the surrounding swamp, her eye looking for the swishing tails and rippled backs of the alligators who may be closing in on the fresh meat.

Shank looped one arm around the girl's waist and turned her face-up; an angry gash was cut into her head, wrapping from her forehead to her left ear. Her blue eyes were wide open, never blinking out the dirty water.

Maria's hand flew to her mouth and she crouched onto her knees on the dock.

"Pull her up," Shank said as they gripped the dock with one hand and villagers began to aid. Two men helped lift the girl out of the water, laying her on her back across the floating walkway.

The little boy sank to his knees, cupping the girl's face in his hands.

"F... Firefly!" He wept, clutching his sister as she lay still.

Shank pulled themself up onto the dock, wasting no time in kneeling next to the boy. They smoothed his hair and held a hand on his shoulder, trying anything he could to soothe the child.

"Cricket, did you see what happened? Was this an accident?"

The child nodded, tears and snot running down his face as he sobbed.

"Our... the... the house just fell!"

Shank looked at Maria so that the boy wouldn't see the suspecting narrow of his eyes. She didn't have to be told twice what they were thinking: someone had intentionally done this, and she knew exactly why. A fate that had been meant for the ill-loved leader of Wrencrest had fallen upon his daughter.

"Maria, you have to heal her."

She froze, looking at Shank with pure terror.

"But she's already dead and if I do that, she'll become an unholy body and her spirit will not rest. I could be haunted for the rest of my life," even in a dream, she knew exactly what would befall her.

"Maria, you have to heal her," they said again with the same expression and same tone, the beginning of a looping record stuck on the most awful chord.

"Maria, you have to heal her."

"Maria, you have to heal her."

"Maria, she's going to die."

"Maria, you have to die."

Maria thrust upwards violently from her sleep, wasting no time to notice that it was still the middle of the night before she began to cry. She kicked off the cloak that had covered her like a blanket and pulled her knees up to her chest to rest her head upon while she whimpered quietly.

Movement stirred from behind her and Maria quickly wiped her tears with the back of her sleeve before looking back. Lily looked back at her, sitting up with her arms propped behind her and a look of concern on her face.

"You've been thrashing around. Are you alright?" Lily whispered just loud enough for Maria to hear.

"Did I wake you?"

Lily shook her head when Maria whispered back. "Never been a sound sleeper. Bad dreams?"

Maria paused, trying to think of what to say and not let the tears break free from her eyes again. "No... I just, it's something I-"

"You don't have to say anything. Do you want to stay up a while?"

Maria nodded.

Lily looked down at Avery sleeping on the other side of her in the campfire circle, tangled up in her own cloak and breathing steadily through an open mouth. Lily pursed her lips like she was stifling back a laugh and carefully rose to her feet, sitting down again beside Maria.

"Lay back down and make yourself comfortable, it'll make it easier to fall back asleep," she instructed kindly.

Maria was too tired to argue and laid back down with her back to Lily, too embarrassed to let her see her face. With one quick peek over her shoulders, Maria looked at Lily. She didn't expect to be met with a soft smile, Lily put a reassuring hand on Maria's shoulder only for a short moment and Maria turned back around with reddened cheeks.

"Don't worry, I won't tell anyone about this. I'll move as soon as you're fast asleep," Lily whispered even quieter as Maria was closing her eyes.

As long as there was kindness in this world, Maria knew she would at least be okay. For another day.

CHAPTER FIVE
THE WHEEL OF FORTUNE

They traversed through the trees in silence as Ina carved out a route with her snout low to the ground. The sun was suddenly blocked as a long shadow stretched over Avery.

"This is just about the place," the velveteen voice spoke. She whirled around with a startled gasp and looked up at the looming figure that was the demon of the crossroads.

"Don't hate me for this, daughter," Balthazar spoke again but his words nor his expression seemed to hold any sincere remorse.

Avery panicked and tried to make sense of the words, opening her mouth to demand clarification until the shifting of the earth beneath her feet turned her words into a scream. Her friends around her hollered in protest as the solid earth became water under her weight.

"*The bastard! Don't let go of me, Avery.*"

She squeezed Aegis in her arms a little tighter than she should have as she plunged through the surface of the earth, the darkness swallowing her, and the cat's body vanished. *Hadn't the bastard cat just said to hold on?*

The dirt would fill her mouth and every last corner of her lungs until she suffocated; she knew it. The earth in her eardrums would block out any sound from above that somehow made it down below. She would die alone in a dark world of silence, undoubtedly.

Who Reaps a Reaper? Maybe that was what Balthazar had just done. Don't hate him? *I'm going to fucking haunt him!*

But the suffocation never came. Avery was still able to heave a panicked pant. She could have sworn she heard someone call her name as she fell through, air? It was a tunnel!

Avery reached out one arm slowly with an open hand and found that she was indeed falling. Moving air hit her downward palms as she stretched a little further to find the tunnel walls of dirt. Her fingers grasped at the dirt, trying to grab ahold of anything to stop her from falling further into nothingness.

And if she did manage to stop, what would she do then? Climb her way back to the top? She felt she must have been falling for hours and the certainty of death numbed her.

"Avery!"

Her name was called out from somewhere above her and echoed down at her from somewhere in the narrow burrow. Was that Moz? The voice was too warped to tell. Another voice spoke much clearer.

"*Avery, calm down.*"

Aegis? Her throat burned as she mustered up energy to call out with a croaked voice.

"Wh... where are you?"

The air in the tunnel filled her mouth with stale dust and Avery's body jerked as she mentally willed herself not to go into a coughing fit but failed.

"*We're waiting for you at the bottom. Fall feet first. Moz is close behind.*"

She nodded even though she knew Aegis couldn't see her, or so she had assumed. Who else was with him?

Avery tucked her arms as close to her torso as she could, straightening out her flailing legs as Aegis had instructed. She fell for what felt like minutes before she saw a faint green glow beneath her feet. Surely her mind was playing tricks on her in the darkness. Before she could think of any possible sources for the eerie light, a mouth of green swallowed her and she crumpled into a heap on a hard surface. Rolling onto her stomach, she felt every bone in her body had shattered under sudden impact.

Avery gasped for air in stuttered chokes with closed eyes. If she wasn't dead before, she must have been now.

She willed her eyelids to open and was surprised when they fluttered without a fight. Her head spun with dizziness and a moment passed before she realized she was staring at a pair of black boots standing on a jagged cobblestone ground. She struggled to suck in a breath of air; wherever she landed was disgustingly humid and had a rank scent of rot.

"Damn, that had to hurt," a voice bright with youth said from somewhere behind her.

Who was that?

"Up we go, now. Od Welcoming Committee here to help," Aegis said, and she saw a pair of clawed hands reach down for her. Avery shrieked and the hands recoiled as though her reaction startled whoever they belonged to.

A heavy thud to the ground came from somewhere out of her stuck line of vision followed by an annoyed groan. That was, without a doubt, Moz; the smaller voice must have been Jack.

"Aren't either of you going to help her up," Moz snapped and a different set of hands grabbed onto her biceps, one of the wrists inked opaque black underneath the hem of a dark sleeve. A glimmer of relief glowed in her panic; Moz was here. There was a strange but warm safety in his grip.

He slowly helped Avery up onto her feet and every bone in her body pleaded for her to lay back down. Her eyes widened when she came face to face with the demon she had been living with since her Inception as a Reaper.

Aegis was equally as tall as Moz but somehow even more spindly and spider-like. The eyes that stared back at her held inky black sclera and golden irises under heavy eyebrows. The copper flush of his skin reflected the otherworldly green that hung heavy over wherever it was they were - did Aegis say Od?

Aegis lifted his hands and she once more saw the claws stretching out from his fingers, easily several inches long. He grinned and Avery saw that his teeth were just as unnervingly sharp.

"Not so cute and cuddly anymore, am I?" Aegis' dagger-like claws clinked together as he wiggled them.

Next to Aegis, Jack looked up at him with a skeptical raise of his black eyebrows that didn't fit the blonde hair on the rest of his head. The demon boy looked like she imagined Kurosaki might have in his teen years, right down to the fur-trimmed hood of his parka. His white hair and pupil-less eyes glinted green under the radioactive sky.

"As much as I would love to sit here and mock your appearance, we really need to find Mona's spell book," Moz said in a low voice before looking towards Avery. "You're neither dead nor a demon, but I think I have a plan to keep you hidden from the demons who would maul you if they see your heartbeat. I don't think you're gonna like it though."

"See my heartbeat?"

She looked down in confusion and saw the orange glow through her black shirt, emanating from within her ribcage. Panicked, she held a hand over her heart, but it beat just as ordinarily as it did in the land of the living. Avery pulled her cloak in around herself in an attempt to hide it, but the warm light penetrated the heavy fabric as well.

"What do we have to do?" Her voice trembled and she tried to keep quiet as though the denizens of the underworld could hear her over their own echoing cackles of laughter.

"You're as bright as a lighthouse! You'll blend in if we can hide your heartbeat. You stand in the middle of us and we'll all cover you as much as we can," Jack spoke softly, knowing exactly what his Reaper intended to do.

Aegis laughed once with sarcastic vitriol. "Ha! You really think making an Avery sandwich is going to keep them from pouncing on us?"

"Feel free to grace us with your superior idea," Moz snapped back.

Aegis only grinned a toothy smile, perhaps satisfied with his ability to grind on Moz's nerves, but he offered no alternative solution. "Alright. Form a triangle around her."

Jack was the first to flank Avery. "You should keep armed, y'know, just in case."

Avery nodded and she fumbled to draw her sword, doubtful that Jack would even be able to shield her with his short stature. He stood eye to eye with her and a grim fog began swirling in his empty orbital spheres as she watched him. Shadows and shapes began to emerge in the white nothingness before Moz gently grabbed her by the elbow to turn her gaze away.

"You don't want to be doing that," he said. He turned around with his blade drawn forward, inching backwards so that he could lead the smashed group. Jack's face turned outward and away from Avery when he flanked her right side, but she could almost hear the pout in his voice when he spoke.

"I wasn't going to hurt her!"

She felt the point of Aegis' boot toe pressed up against her heel as he protected her back and left side. Avery's muscles went rigid when the demons enclosed her with their bodies and she tightened her grip around Hemlock to reassure herself. Jack wasn't going to hurt her, or so he said. Aegis probably had finding the spell book in his best interest and would at least be courteous enough to not kill her until they had found it. And Moz. The caress across her cheek was almost as real as the one she recalled - he wouldn't hurt her.

"Go on," Aegis hissed, urging them to move.

Their disjointed shuffling was awkward and out of sync before they walked several yards and a unanimous pace was understood. Avery peered through the spaces between their shoulders to get a good look at Od.

The windows of the buildings seemed to peer back at her as though they were the eyes of the broken and bent faces. Their sidings were peeling and chipping beneath pediment statues of macabre funeral processions. She looked up to try to find the source of the sickly, green atmosphere but it could have been coming from anywhere. A fog? Marine blankets of mist had rolled into Ardua many times, but it was nothing like the dense cloud hanging over their heads.

The avenue they walked on was almost as narrow as the tunnel Avery had fallen through but it was eerily empty. She held her breath for a moment and prayed that they wouldn't encounter anyone else during their task.

"Do any of you actually know where we're supposed to be going," she whispered to the group when she finally let go of the breath.

"There is a building in the center of the Necropolis that I believe might contain the spell book we need. A vault, if you will," Aegis said. "However, I'm not sure what to expect as far as guards are concerned. If Balthazar said that they're on the watch for him to retrieve it, I imagine that we cannot simply stroll inside. There is a good chance She already knows we're here."

Avery swallowed hard. "I'm not so sure that I'm confident in the outcome anymore."

The cacophonous chatter Avery had only just become aware of grew louder as they shuffled deeper into the Necropolis. She caught glimpses of horned skulls, endless rows of eyeballs, and grotesque teeth as the narrow avenue became more populated with the denizens of Od. Her heart raced and she looked down at the light within her ribcage glowing brighter under the folds of her cloak.

Avery walked as closely as she could to Moz's back in hopes that it would reduce her chances of being spotted. When she ducked her head down her forehead pressed against the rough fabric of his coat and she followed purely through her sense of touch. For a moment she wondered if she should grab his hand that hung so calmly at his side.

One fear overcame another and Avery grabbed hold of Moz's fingers. At first, she expected him to shrug out of the frightened grip, but he gave her hand a reassuring squeeze. They began to travel down a winding hill, their shuffling becoming staggered once again until they regained a rhythm.

"Keep cool," Moz suddenly said and Avery barely stopped herself from asking for clarification.

"WILLIAM!"

A deep scratch of a voice bellowed from somewhere in front of their cluster of bodies and Avery did not dare to look up to see who, or what, it belonged to. The familiarity with Moz was unnerving enough for her.

"Nice to see you, Teeth," Moz returned a greeting at a much more reasonable volume and Avery made sure to *definitely* not look at whatever demon had a name like "Teeth". Moz stopped for the conversation and she halted just in time to avoid smacking hard into his backside when he let go of her hand. She didn't realize just how comforting it had been until his fingers were unlaced from hers and her anchor to the living was gone.

"Jackie boy, it's been too long since seeing you," the demon carried on. "But what are you doing here, Aegis? I thought you were a familiar?"

Oh gods, here it comes. Avery held her breath as though the smallest exhale might give away her location, dipping her head even lower as she stared at their feet on the cobbles. How in the world was this working?

"The operative word is 'was'," Aegis answered with a cool demeanor. "I killed her."

Oh, for fuck's sake. Teeth heaved with thick mucus and what was probably a laugh. Avery saw Moz shift on his feet as though the sound made even him uncomfortable.

"Reapers, what are you going to do about 'em," Teeth chuckled before adding "No offense, William."

"None taken. We should really get going, Teeth."

"Where are you going all tangled up like a rat king? HA! Get it, Will?"

Jack snickered next to her and Avery made every effort not to prod him in the ribs to quiet him. Luckily Moz ignored Teeth entirely and began walking again, Aegis and Jack following with Avery inside.

"See you around, Teeth," Jack chimed. "Get it? You have no eyes."

This time Avery really did prod Jack, causing him to flinch and she instantly wished she hadn't when she was exposed. Jack caught his slip quickly and snapped back into formation to cover her. Teeth only laughed heartily at the flat joke and the demon boy beamed proudly as they passed. Avery let herself exhale in relief.

She dared herself to look up and behind her before Teeth was out of sight. A head of red, leathery flesh easily towered high enough for her to see from inside her barrier of bodies. Teeth was undoubtedly tall enough to see into their huddle and yet he seemed completely unaware of Avery's presence. Jack said that he had no eyes, but the demon was able to pick the three of them out from the crowd even without them.

"He doesn't have eyes, though we can sense the unique signature of each demon," Aegis clarified as though he could somehow hear her thoughts. Could he? "Obviously, you don't have one. We got lucky that time, but we'll have to be more careful. Don't leave your post, Jack."

Each demon had a unique signature. She remembered Aegis mentioning something about sensing signatures in the forest outside of Ardua, but back then she didn't think it applied to them. Avery turned and looked at up at him.

"And that's how you knew Moz had the Knight?"

"Exactly how."

Avery frowned. "Why didn't you mention this before? You know, upon meeting?"

Aegis shrugged. "Cat, curiosity, blah, blah."

"Cat bastard."

Lily stared in horror at the spot on the ground where Avery had slipped through; Moz had dove in after her as though it were merely water. Not far from it was the limp body of Aegis and the small rat Moz kept with him.

She scrambled towards the spot, frantically shoveling dirt with her hands to dig her way to wherever they had vanished. Lily screamed out in frustration, the grit of the earth was easily working its way beneath her short fingernails and drawing blood. Panicked tears pricked in her eyes and a slight burn sat in the lip of her bottom eyelids as the salt mixed with what remained of her mascara.

She looked back up and quickly grabbed her bow from where she had thrown it on the ground, drawing towards the strange man who had appeared out of thin air.

"Where did you send them," she demanded through gritted teeth as she rose back to her feet, her aim wavering with nerves.

He only smiled at her with a rather patronizing tilt of the head. The crow that had been perched on the shoulder of his waistcoat cried out sharply before taking off into the sky; even the bird didn't want to see what Lily was about to do to this man.

"I must say," he spoke slowly with a rich voice and Lily shivered with the eerie memories of Morgana. "I have never been threatened by a human before. I've been haggled with, been pitied, and been feared. But never been threatened by one. I like you."

Lily inched backwards to where she knew Maria was standing without ever taking her aim off the creepy man. When Lily was next to Maria, she leaned to the side to be heard even in a quiet voice.

"Who is this guy?" Lily hissed through her teeth.

"Balthazar," Maria explained in a soft voice. "He's the one we bring the souls to. He sends them to the gods or to Od. Keeper of the Crossroads."

Lily swallowed hard. Of all the people she could have been aiming at, her target was the ultimate gatekeeper. She found herself wishing that this whole other world Avery had just proven to her was mere myth again; that there was nothing overtly fantastic about the way people died and where they went after the fact. Lily found herself bracing for the million-year nap as she stared into the face of the grinning gatekeeper.

"Well, no going back now," she joked nervously to Maria before straightening her stance with the arrow still pointed at Balthazar. Lily knew shooting him would probably have no effect, but if she lowered her bow they would stand even less of a chance should Balthazar decide to attack them.

Lily did her best to ignore the burning fear in her belly. Perhaps she was already facing death, but she knew she might as well keep being tough.

"Where did you send them," she repeated.

"Put down the bow. You're shaking like a leaf and it makes it rather difficult to take you seriously," Balthazar said instead of answering her.

Lily's glance slid down for a moment to her arms and she saw that he was right. Whether it was by exhaustion or by fear, she was quivering intensely.

She lowered her bow but the tension did not fade. Balthazar stepped forward, his black eyes sliding up and down Lily as though to assess whether she might have been a threat. He lifted his hand, covered in gaudy rings, and scratched at the short beard on his chin in an exaggerated gesture of thought. Finally he smiled, to Lily's further discomfort.

"I have a gift for you. Accept it and I will tell you."

Lily raised an eyebrow in skepticism. "Why a gift? What is it?"

"You don't ask questions. You take it."

A hand grabbed her by the arm and yanked her backwards. She whirled around and stood at a breath's reach from Maria. A warm flush brightened her cheeks as though she didn't mean to pull Lily so close, but she didn't step back either.

"Remember Avery and the spirits? That was a gift from Balthazar. You need to really think about this," she murmured.

"I don't think we really have a choice on this. We don't know if Avery and Moz will come back alive."

Maria was silent for a moment, her eyes flickering as though she was studying her face while trying to come up with a rebuttal. She took in a small breath like she was trying to prepare; as though she was the one who was bartering with Balthazar.

"Just be careful," she warned.

Lily nodded before turning back around. Balthazar was looking rather impatient, pretending to look at an invisible pocket watch. He mimed shoving it back into his coat pocket before tilting his head once more.

"Are we done deliberating?"

"I'll take it," she stated firmly, hoping she would not come to regret it.

Balthazar smiled widely and straightened out his long, hunched over body. He lifted his right arm, folding back the cuff of his coat neatly before repeating the same exaggerated action on his left cuff. Lily's heart pounded after noticing the action was like a surgeon snapping on gloves. What was he going to do to her?

"I think you'll find that you made the right decision. I'm actually excited for you," he said before quickly closing the distance she made sure to keep between them.

He took both palms and forced them flat against each of Lily's temples, holding her head in his calloused hands. A shrill hiss rang in her ears on contact and her eardrums buzzed in pain. She shrieked, dropping her bow and buckling at the knees. Balthazar's lips moved as he looked down on her, but she couldn't make out any words over the droning screech in her skull.

Her hands instinctively reached up to try to pry his hands away from her flesh, but a pair of hands slid onto her fingers and held her fast. Small and soft, she could only assume that it was Maria who had stopped her. Why was no one else helping her?

The smell of burning metal overcame her nostrils and flooded her other senses, just as tortuous as the shrill screeching. A warm sensation dribbled over her philtrum and a coppery taste glided onto her lips. Lily panicked even further at the realization of her bleeding nose; what was he doing to her?

"STOP!"

His hands dropped her with a sudden jerk and Balthazar lurched backwards in the air as though pushed; Maria's hands were yanked away from her own. Her ears ached even after the ringing was gone and she looked in astonishment at the sudden distance between her and Balthazar. His face was not painted with horror, but rather satisfaction.

"That should give you a little more of an edge," he said, brushing dirt off the front of his black waistcoat.

Lily wiped the blood from her face with the back of her hand and looked down at the smear with horror.

"Wha- what did you do to me?"

"I've made you the ultimate sharpshooter! How can you possibly miss when your mind is so strong, daughter? Look at your bow on the ground and lift it without moving a single finger."

His suddenly jovial demeanor only added to Lily's fright. She turned to look at Maria for help just as she was picking herself off the ground. Maria wiped blood away from her bottom lip with the back of her hand, the blood on her front teeth as she bit her lip hard enough to draw blood. Did Lily throw her, too?

"Maria, I'm sorry, I—"

Lily couldn't help but look at the bow on the ground, Balthazar's command too fresh in her mind to simply ignore. The weapon rattled on the ground by its own volition and was tossed aside by seemingly nothing. Lily knotted her fingers in her hair, buckling forward at the knees in her panic.

"WHAT DID YOU DO TO ME," she screamed again.

Balthazar's tone became solemn and calm as he approached her. "It is act of manipulating your surroundings only by wishing to do so. Your mind is your best tool, daughter. You accepted an uncertainty for the good of those important to you, despite the fear. That is very admirable. For that I can promise you this will help, not harm. And so I tell you to wait."

"W…wait?"

"Wait," he repeated. "They must leave the way they came, through the vent I opened for them. While it is sealed up here, it is open and a passage from where they are: Od."

"I DID THIS AND YOU TELL ME TO WAIT?"

As Lily screamed furiously, the bow became airborne once more in Balthazar's direction. The Keeper of the Crossroads vanished before he could be struck, the bow falling to the ground just beyond where he had been standing. He did not return, leaving them in weary silence.

— 🕊 —

"Is this really the place?"

Avery peeked from behind Moz to look at the building they had stopped at. It stood tall on top of a massive set of marble stairs, shadows cast from the titanic columns on the porch hid the entrance. The pediment adorning the top was much like the ones Avery had seen over and over during their shuffled journey: a funeral procession of weeping women and children. She couldn't help but notice that there were no demons nor dead souls anywhere to be seen; the vault was remarkably unguarded.

"It is," Aegis answered simply. The lack of any sentinels must have been usual as he did not sound at all perplexed.

"Shouldn't it be guarded?"

Aegis chuckled when she voiced her concern, making her even more nervous.

"That's not the Beldam's style. Why put up guards that can be cut down when instead you can hide something far more sinister? No, what waits for us inside will be much worse than a few guards."

"Wow, you truly are a comfort to all," Avery snapped with biting sarcasm, even though she knew it wasn't Aegis' fault there wasn't any need for guards posted.

It wasn't the promise of something waiting to claim their lives that terrified Avery, but the fact that it was a thing unknown to even Aegis. She had no way of even *beginning* to imagine what the goddess of the underworld could concoct.

Moz looked up the giant staircase; even he was hesitant to face whatever was waiting for them. He reached behind his shoulder, unsheathing his sword.

"Are you ready, Avery?"

She nodded when he looked back at her. They began their ascent and Avery felt exposed; Jack barely shielded the glow of her heartbeat from the dead world around them. Aegis noticed and urged them forward with a quicker pace and by skipping steps.

"We can't cover Avery, we need to run," he hissed.

No sooner than Aegis had pointed out the hazard, a screech came from somewhere behind them.

"A heart!"

Avery could not stop herself from looking behind her and past Jack at the one-eyed demon pointing a bony claw in their direction. Other demons followed his stare; their lips snarled with hungry growls. She was frozen in place despite every instinct telling her to run and she couldn't break her stare at the mass of monsters running towards the steps.

Moz grabbed her by the arm, dragging her up the steps. He yelled something that she didn't comprehend until the fear gave way to her need to survive. She sprinted after Moz and the demons to the top of the stairs, the shadows cast by the columns embraced them with darkness that she wished was dense enough to protect them from the beasts below.

"In here!"

Jack ran towards a set of white doors, pushing one open with his boot and holding it open for the rest of them to follow. Avery couldn't see inside the building it led to, but she doubted the gnashing teeth of the demons left her much of a choice.

She dashed inside with Aegis and Moz close behind, a clawed hand on her shoulder shoving her into the dark room. Moz slammed the door shut as he was the last to enter and pressed against it as though to barricade the entry with only his body weight before they were shrouded in darkness. There was a whirring of tumblers and spinning gears as the door locked itself.

"Err… should we be concerned about that?" Jack said of the self-locking door.

An eerie humidity hung heavy in the air and Avery realized that they had potentially ran from one danger into the mouth of another. The warm glow of her heart reached only inches around her before being swallowed by the thick darkness. She flinched as a cacophony of fists banged on the other side of the door, demanding to be let inside. Her heart raced as she stepped away from the door and stopped when she realized that she had no idea what else was in the room.

"What do we do now," she whispered, afraid of who or what might also have been listening.

"Avery, be our lantern," Jack suggested jokingly.

Avery's uneasy laugh was only a forced exhale. She heard a shuffling of movement in the blackness from somewhere in front of her followed by the satisfying strike of a match. The small flame lit Moz's face as he held it between his fingers.

"Find something to light, she must have left something in here so we could at least see our impending doom."

Avery managed to chuckle nervously that time, "I kind of hate all of you right now."

She inched towards where she thought the door was, her hands held out in front of her. Avery's fingers touched a damp stone wall and she shivered in disgust.

With her hands still anchoring her to the wall, she walked sideways and searched for anything to create a bigger fire.

Avery could have heard the grimace on Aegis' face with his sharp snap back. "Why me? I could have left you for dead your very first *hour* outside of Ardua. Foolish girl, you wouldn't have found the riv-"

"I found a torch on the wall!" Jack called out from somewhere to Avery's right.

The flame in Moz's hand disappeared as he turned towards Jack, mumbling before a torch ignited and illuminated the room in a warm glow.

The chamber that they stood in was far more expansive than Avery had initially thought; the echoes of their argument had not just been in her imagination. The same cold marble that adorned the facade of the building made up the windowless walls of the room. The only door was the one they had just passed through.

On the other side of the room was a simple pedestal with an even simpler wooden box sitting on top of it. *Is Mona's spell book inside?* Surely it should have been more difficult to get to. Her eyes slid to the small grey mountain laying on the floor just beyond it, its surface reflecting the torch light in small glints. It was so close to the color of the walls that Avery could have easily missed it.

"Oh no," Aegis grumbled. "I see where this is going."

"The spell book is in that box, right? We just grab it and go," she asked nervously as she turned to look back at him.

Jack shook his head, his white eyes wide with fear as he raised a pointed finger towards the grey mass. "That's an elslith right there."

Avery whirled back around with Hemlock raised in front of her. "What... is it?"

Moz held his sword up, stepping cautiously towards whatever the thing was. He held up one finger to signal for them to be silent as he crept closer. The closer his tall frame got to the elslith, the clearer it was as to why the chamber was eerily vast: to house the grey giant.

"It appears to be dormant for now," Moz called out. "I don't think it will stay that way once we open the box."

Aegis turned and looked at her with a stern stare. "Avery, you stay back here while we get the book."

Avery pulled her face in an insulted frown. "Fuck you, I'm getting it."

No way am I letting him tell me what to do! She trudged towards the pedestal before Aegis could physically stop her. Avery had almost made it halfway before he called out after her.

"You know, calling upon the spirits won't work here."

Avery stopped in her tracks. She couldn't lie to herself and say that her strength didn't come from the spirits; she wasn't a fool. That big of one, anyway.

Without them she knew she would not have enough strength to fight whatever the elslith was. But if she didn't get the spell book, what would happen? To Lily, to Moz, to her adopted family, to her birth parents, to everyone she ever knew.

She stepped forward slower than before, holding her sword in front of her more cautiously. Avery expected Moz to stop her but as he did in the Temple of Centralia, he trusted her to fight. She was again reminded of the faith he had in her, even after all the things he had ever said or did to make her think otherwise. *That had to count for something, right?* Moz wasn't one to have blind faith, especially when lives were on the line.

When she approached the box, she lifted her left hand from Hemlock's grip, reaching slowly to open it. She looked to her left at Moz, who watched not her but the elslith with a ready sword. Avery swallowed hard. Nothing bad could happen to her. Not like this, not with three demons on her side.

She flipped the metal latch and the box flew open as though it contained an erupting volcano, black smoke violently poured from inside. It shot upwards towards the vaulted ceiling, revealing a brown leather book beneath where the smoke had laid waiting inside of the box. Avery hurriedly grabbed it, cradling it with her left arm and watching the smoke as she scrambled backwards. Its black form swirled in the air before hurtling down at the elslith and vanishing into the mass of grey flesh.

Bones sighed and groaned as it stirred with movement, the nooks and crannies along its flanks unfolding into hideous limbs. Arms and legs of mismatching proportions stretched out along the bottom of the grey mass, eyes blinking to life on all sides of the elslith. Shadows of faces appeared faintly under the translucent flesh with their mouths contorted into screams. They snapped their jaws underneath the membrane as though to chew their way out but were unable to put flesh between their teeth.

On the side of the elslith closest to Moz, the pale flesh parted into a mouth to reveal jagged rows of teeth and viscous saliva. A stench of decay quickly overcame the room, but Avery was far too horrified by the sight to worry about the smell.

"The elslith are made from the bodies of humans sent to Od," Aegis explained calmly from somewhere behind Avery. "Plucked by the Beldam and smashed together to serve whatever purpose She desires. It looks as though in this case, a more threatening vessel for the demon in that box."

Avery quickly shoved the book into her rucksack as she watched Moz begin to backpedal cautiously, his white blade held in front of him as the beast reared backwards to rise on its dozens of back limbs. Unlike his Reaper, Jack stepped towards the elslith; pulling out a long dagger from underneath his black parka with eyes focused on the belly of the beast.

"Avery, keep as far away from the mouth as you can," Moz called out. "You and I both know you can use Hemlock well enough, but this isn't the time to take any chances. Get him from behind."

The elslith slung its worm-like head from side to side until its body curled and stretched back outwards with a stabbing roar that briefly disoriented Avery. Then came the first strike, its gnashing teeth aiming first at Moz. He dashed out of the elslith's path and the beast traveled several yards before realizing there was no prey to be held in its jaws.

The beast roared again and Avery cupped her hands over her ears to block out as much sound as she could. She realized that she didn't recall seeing any eyes on the elslith; was it looking for them by sound? The chamber was so vast that reverberating sound couldn't have possibly revealed where they were standing, but with a creature so otherworldly Avery couldn't rule anything out.

Avery dropped her hands and quickly followed the tail end of the elslith. She grimaced when she heard a sickening squish of the slime underneath her boot, pulling her foot out with some resistance from the viscous fluid.

The beast roared again and snapping back to focus, she wielded her sword protectively in front of her.

Avery swung it down on the grey flesh, a shameful portion of her burst of energy fueled by the desire to rid the air of the rancid stench of decay. The skin was punctured and clear plasma splattered to the stone floor. It was not Avery who cried out in displeasure, but Jack.

"We've got a problem!"

She looked higher up the left flank of the elslith to where Jack was standing with one arm coated in ooze, pointing at the wound in the ghostly flesh quickly sealing itself back up. Where the flesh of one eaten body was ruined, another filled its place. Her face contorted with dread, looking at Aegis as though he would have a solution.

The demon was only paces behind Moz as he whistled a seconds-long tune before pausing to step elsewhere; luring the elslith by sound. Moz slashed at the oozing face, looking at Aegis with an enraged scowl, furious that the demon wasn't assisting more.

"We're going to need something bigger," Aegis called out. "If you know what I mean, Moz."

Everyone ignored Jack's snickering. He was cut off by a screech from the elslith, no doubt the beast was growing frustrated and looking for the prey that had crept into its lair. Moz looked from Aegis to the elslith, an uneasy frown on his face as he backpedaled carefully. She could see it in his expression: he didn't have much of a choice and knew he must transform into the Knight.

Without taking his eyes off the slithering beast, who had just turned its massive head towards them, he spoke to Avery in a low voice to avoid drawing the elslith in.

"Avery, you and the Knight get us all out of here. We have to go through the same tunnel we fell through. Kill it if you can, but getting you out is more important if we already have the book."

"I will."

Aegis and Jack sprinted away from Moz as he bent at the knees, wanting to be as far away from him as they could when he collapsed into the Knight. Adrenaline pumped hard in her blood not from fear, but the otherworldly cracking of bones and the flap of wings belonging to the beast born of only a man.

The Knight unhinged its skeletal jaw in a sharp roar, the elslith reeling backwards in astonishment at the sudden wall of sound that it had not created. The elslith's sense of echolocation had been thrown off, Avery hoped, and it swung its head side to side as it screeched to try to regain its sense of the space.

Once more she felt a pulling sensation, the unseen lure that the Knight used to call upon her. This time, her fear was lessened by knowing what the sensation from the battle at Centralia was and she waved the other demons to follow her as she maneuvered towards the flank of the Knight that was furthest from the elslith.

The creature reared back, sitting upright on one of the many mismatching human limbs, shrieking as it tried to dominate the Knight with sheer sound. It jabbed in the Reaper's direction with gnashing teeth, cut off when the Knight rammed back with its skeletal head and pierced the gooey flesh with its horn.

"Hurry!"

Avery called out as she grabbed hold of the exposed rib cage, her boots slipping once before she was able to scale the side. She wedged herself between two of the horns running down the demon's spine, patting the rucksack on her back to reassure herself that she still had the spell book in her possession.

Jack had barely managed to straddle the spine of the Knight before the ground disappeared from beneath them. With the demonic beast airborne in the vast chamber, Aegis still clung onto the side with his clawed hands closed around two rib bones. Her heart leaped in her throat and she squeezed the hilt of Hemlock in her right hand.

"He's going to ram down the door!"

Jack's voice was barely heard over the frustrated screeching of the elslith. She trusted his judgement, knowing Jack had been in Moz's head just before he gave way to the Knight.

The Knight flew up into the farthest corner of the chamber before diving at the pair of doors they had entered from. With its head tilting down, the Knight rammed the door against the flat of its enormous skull and the doors erupted in an explosion of warped metal and broken tumblers. Bodies of the demons that had lingered at the door of the vault were knocked aside, weighing nothing compared to the force of the titanic beast. Bones crunched from somewhere behind them as the elslith chewed its way through the horde of demons the Knight did not already plow through.

A wall of screeching and roaring hit them as the Knight ricocheted off a building, sending ceramic shingles crashing in every direction before launching into the air. With both hands gripping a bone tightly, Avery dared herself to turn around to look behind them.

Past Jack's morbidly exuberant face she saw the elslith catching up rather quickly, rearing up with snapping teeth - dripping remnants of demons' flesh snagged between the grey daggers. Too many times, Avery found, it came close to closing its jaws around the Knight's skeletal tail.

"Can't we get any higher?"

Avery's voice could not be heard over the disastrous sounds around her and she looked up, finding that the land of the dead had a rather unusual ceiling. While she knew it was foolish to expect a sky, she was still surprised to see the impenetrable layer of earth with tangled tree roots, trapping the denizens of Od in their hell. Off in the distance, she caught sight of a hole in the ceiling of solid dirt: *the tunnel!*

The Knight jerked violently as its tail was clipped by the head of the elslith. Jack's hand grabbed onto her shoulder hard as she shook, as though he could keep her steady with just one hand. With a swoop of her arm, she drew Hemlock. She would be ready the next time. Avery looked behind them through locks of hair flapping in the violent wind.

Beneath them were rows upon rows of jagged teeth, the open throat of the elslith revealing the faces of the damned humans with sickening clarity. She thought for a moment she heard their warped cries for help. Terror froze her and a sublime fear of the monster gripped her every bone.

The elslith was nearly upon them when the present snapped back to her- the shouts of Aegis and Jack heard again, the wind from the flapping wings of the Knight. Avery let out a guttural scream with the final blow, putting every ounce of force she had behind the drive of her sword into the face of the elslith. The beast reeled backwards in surprise and the distance between the two monsters immediately stretched further.

When she ripped her sword back out of the ghastly flesh, she had expected the wound to drip the clear plasma, but it bled a black smoke. Avery watched the smoke terrified confusion, swearing it rose as the elslith sank to the ground of the Necropolis. Before she could wholly realize the smoke was zipping towards them, she slipped backwards with a sudden blow to the skull and the world of the dead slipped away from around her.

CHAPTER SIX

THE MOON

Yumi knew that the tavern wasn't a place for women like her. Not because of the exaggerated acts of aggression demonstrated by the men of Brightloch, but the spirits that hung around them. The lingering dead knew she could see them and hear their whispering voices, and they'd be damned if they didn't make sure she heard everything they had to say. She feared that the disguise, which was more of an oversized cloak than a disguise at all, would not work as well on the dead as it would on the living.

She felt Mara stir against her hipbone in the sling she wore across the front of her body, mildly comforted by the reminder that the rabbit was still there. Yumi slipped deeper into the dim tavern, her gaze slid from head to head of the men sitting at the long wooden tables; she was confident they wouldn't see her staring with the hood of her brown cloak pulled low over her face. She looked ahead of her and caught sight of what she had really come there for.

At the other end of the tavern was a board haphazardly covered in town notices, calls for work, and wanted posters. She came to see specifically one of them. Yumi pushed past a man obscuring most of the walkway, paying no mind to whatever it was he had been saying.

Yumi scanned the board quickly, her heart racing when she stopped upon the exact face she was hoping to see.

They had ignored her freckles, made her eyes far too small. The Berserker Witch's face - *no, Avery's face.* It was important that Yumi never lost sight of the humanity belonging to her, no matter how foul the mouths of gossipers painted her to be.

Berserker Witch! Wanted: For Murder, Treason, and Necromancy. Was the headline even to be believed?

Beside Avery's poster was a rendering of a man she had recognized from the memories Owen had showed her. Without the blood smeared on his face, Yumi might not have recognized him had it not been for the long waves of hair atop his head, shaved shorter on the sides in a rather unusual cut. *William Mosley! Wanted: For Murder, Manslaughter of Government Officials, and Treason.*

She felt a stirring of the thing that lived in the back of her head as he stared back at her, seeming to frown with his scarred eyebrow. Without using words, she knew what the Knight was trying to say: this was her brother in Knighthood. What was William Mosley like? Certainly the accusations against him couldn't be true either, especially if he was travelling with someone like Avery. Yumi doubted she would keep someone like that in her company.

"Ye' lookin for a reward?"

The gruff voice of a man came from behind Yumi and it was then that she noticed the bounties beneath their paper faces. Were their lives worth five hundred coin? She scoffed and turned around to face the man, careful to make sure her hood was still concealing her face.

"What do you know about them? Are they within the city walls?" Yumi asked.

The man scanned her from toes to head with brown eyes, scratching at his ginger beard unkempt and wet with spilled grog. Mara was frozen still at her side, certainly doing her best not to attract attention.

"Not last I heard, y'miss. Coupla men have ventured out to find 'em, never goin' tha' far. 'Specially after hearin' speculation tha' they're headin' this way. The coin'll fall righ' in some lucky bastard's lap!"

"*Checks out with what the boy had said,*" Mara whispered in her head.

"Do you know why?" Yumi asked the man, careful not to miss a beat in the flow of conversation. Careful not to let the blonde maiden with the slit throat know that Yumi could hear anyone besides the man.

The man was ducking at the waist, trying to peer up into Yumi's hood. She backed away and he straightened up, pretending that he had not done such a thing.

"'Sassination attempt on the king, I heard."

"Absurd," Yumi growled with far more anger than she had ever intended on letting on.

She knew for a fact nobody was worrying about her father, she had seen no changes in the royal guard whatsoever. Even more angering was the logic didn't make sense: her father had not left Brightloch in years, and yet the so-called criminals weren't even within the walls. *Would hypothetical assassins enter the city, make the attempt, flee, only to come back?* Whoever came up with the garbage and perpetuated the rumor was insulting the intelligence of every citizen there - apart from this man, apparently.

The man shrugged, not caring to give it another thought. "Beats me, then. All I know is someone'll pay good coin t' bring 'em their heads. I'd rather get these scoundrels than pick off another one of 'em Lost Ones for chump change."

The whispers were true: the humans were picking off the Lost Ones in exchange for money. Yumi had not seen a Lost One for herself but she caught plenty of stories from both the living and the dead.

People were spontaneously transforming into beasts; horns sprouting from their spines, oversized wings unfurling from their backs, teeth unrooting themselves from their gums to make way for piercing fangs - the grotesque possibilities seemed endless. Her father had put up rewards for anyone who brought a dead Lost One to the castle. She had always been ushered out of the hall when a bounty hunter was introduced as successful and had never seen with her own eyes what creature was being dragged inside the castle walls.

She knew the bounty on the Lost Ones was to incentivize hunting them and preventing them from killing any more people, but what could the crown possibly want from Avery and William that was worth so much more than the beasts? There seemed to be so much still that she didn't know about the world she was thrown into.

"I'll pay you double what they are offering to bring them alive. To me."

He stopped laughing, cocking his head curiously to the side. Yumi couldn't help but notice the conversations around them had quieted, her words certainly catching more ears.

"Are y'mad? What could y'possibly want them for? Who are yeh?"

"Do not make that your concern. If and when you find them, I'll know. Tell everyone who you know is looking that the offer stands for them as well. I'll come to you."

Yumi counted on the spirits to tip her off when they were found, she needed to find Avery and William before anyone else did.

— ❦ —

The ground beneath them rumbled and Maria shot up from where she had been sitting idly. Was that an earthquake? They had been waiting for so long that maybe the earth had become impatient as well and was trying to shake the Reapers out of its deepest pits.

"Run!"

Tristan left his rucksack behind and began running, away from the spot where Balthazar said Avery and Moz would be emerging from. Maria connected the information as quickly as she could; it was the Knight!

She ran as fast as she could in the opposite direction to get away, Lily following behind her.

"What's happening?" Lily cried out. Maria had no time to answer before a final impact knocked her off her feet.

The roar of the Knight split the air as chunks of the earth broke free and hurtled in every direction. Maria shielded her eyes from the spray of dirt and uprooted fern, turning to look at the beast as she crawled backwards.

"Oh gods," she heard Lily say breathlessly and Maria still had the same bewildered reaction to seeing the Knight again.

Blue flesh clung to some spots of its skeletal body, the horns on its head trailed down its spine where Maria saw Avery perched and gripping the exposed ribcage. She slid down and landed next to the two men Maria had never seen before, one tall and sinewy while the other was ghostly pale and nearly a child. They were, without a doubt, the true forms of Aegis and Jack.

Avery was backing away as though she did not want to stand near them any longer. The Knight flung off the final bits of earth it brought to the surface by flapping its bat-like wings. It shrunk inwards before imploding into Moz's coughing form, on his hands and knees to spit out the dirt he must have inhaled on the way back up to the surface.

"Moz!" Maria ran to him to help him up.

He accepted the help but between coughs he pointed forward with a single index finger towards Avery.

"Make sure she's okay," he sputtered.

Confused, Maria followed the direction with her gaze. Avery was hunched over on the ground, her back turned towards them with shaking shoulders. Was she laughing? Moz stepped towards her cautiously, lifting a hand as though he were about to place it on her shoulder.

"Avery?"

"Don't come near her," the taller man with black eyes warned, stepping forward but never directly intervening.

The eerie laughter grew louder the longer it carried on and Avery shot up to her feet suddenly. Maria jumped backwards both at the movement and who, or what, she saw when Avery turned around to face them.

The only indication that it wasn't really Avery inhabiting her body was the inky shadows that slowly crept inward from her jawline and formed patches on her exposed hands. Her head was tilted to the side and her mouth was spread in a wide grin. The teeth that overfilled her small mouth weren't hers, but pearlescent daggers.

"I could just kill her right here... right now. Whadda ya think about that, Billy?"

It was Avery's voice, but someone else spoke beneath it; a demon lurked just below the surface of her freckled skin. Maria saw the desperation in Moz's expression, he knew that they couldn't just beat the demon out of Avery. Without taking his eyes off her hunched and sinister form, he spoke to everyone else.

"We need to get Tristan to her. Find a way to restrain her."

Avery laughed with scathing exaggeration as she straightened her neck to stand completely upright. "You have an exorcist with you! I'm hurt, William."

She then turned in the direction of the eldest of the two humanoid familiars. "Aegis, how do you deal with such brats?"

Avery didn't allot time for an answer but instead pulled out the small dagger from her belt before pressing it to her own throat. Moz visibly flinched and Maria jerked forward, stopping short of the demon with hands held up when she realized that she had no intention of grappling with it.

"Don't!"

"I see everything there is to see about Miss Avery Porter, some dark shit, y'know? I bet if you knew the half of it, you would be begging me to cut open her jugular right here and now."

Maria turned to Lily's direction. Her face was stone cold with fury, but Maria could see the subtle shake in her right bicep as she held her bow and arrow at the ready. There was no doubt in Maria's mind that she would have been too terrified to rip the dagger with her mind, not knowing where it would land.

How did it feel to have her weapon pointed at her best friend? Would she actually kill Avery if things went wrong? *Or worse, anyway.* It was only then that Maria remembered she had done the very same thing when Moz had changed into the Knight.

If Maria had blinked, she might have missed Moz take a leap forward, attempting to wrestle the knife out of Avery's fingers. The demon inside her shrieked with glee, throwing Avery's body onto the ground.

"That's right, break every finger on her pathetic, little hands! Kill the witch!"

Avery grabbed Moz by the throat in a flash and her small hand squeezed around his windpipe. Anger boiled in his face as his flesh burned red under her tainted fingers, yet he still fumbled for the knife. Trapping her with his larger frame, he began prying her fingers off the handle of the blade one by one. The demon shrieked and he flinched at the sound.

"You're hurting meeeeeeeeee," she wailed mockingly, the scratching voice of the demon beginning to overcome what was left of Avery's voice.

Maria expected him to falter at the demon's wails, but he succeeded in getting whatever demon was possessing Avery to take the knife away from her throat.

Shank was the one to rip Moz away, both their hands closing around Moz's arm and yanking hard. They pulled him backwards before letting go, looking surprised when they saw the dagger in Moz's open palm. Blood pooled in the cup of flesh from the cuts he received in the fray.

"That's enough," a woman's voice said sharply and everyone's attention shifted. She sat atop a white horse, her body wrapped under a gray cloak. Somehow, they had missed her in all the commotion, even with her bright red hair. It was as though she had appeared as suddenly as the fog that was beginning to blanket the forest floor.

"Morgana," Moz hissed.

Avery laughed and walked backwards towards the horse without taking her eyes off the group. Maria gasped, knowing they had been set up.

"We'll make a deal," Morgana said. "William for the witch."

Avery stood at the neck of the horse, a sinister grin on her face as the inky black began to creep over her nose. She saw Moz's shoulders drop ever so slightly and that was all she needed to know what he was going to do. Maria lifted her own bow and arrow, aiming at Morgana.

"Moz, don't! This is what they want! We'll find another way to free Avery!"

Tristan spoke solemnly next to her. "If we can't exorcise her or get the demon to leave in the next few minutes, Avery will be gone forever. When demons possess living souls, they turn into Beasts."

"Shit!" *No, no, not the angry tears.* Maria felt them burning her cheeks as they fell and she turned her head to protect them from Lily's gaze. Fortunately, she never lifted her aim or focus from Morgana.

Moz turned around, taking off his blessed sword before handing it to Kurosaki. *No, no, no. There has to be another way!*

"We'll find another way around this. You have to find me before they find the last Knight," Moz spoke solemnly as he stepped backwards towards Morgana. "Tell Balthazar what happened here, he will help you. Avery knows how to find him."

He paused for a moment before turning to walk to Morgana head on. "Also Tristan, if you can't save her... his name is Ransom. You'll be responsible for her vengeance and I will forgive you."

Tristan nodded in her peripheral vision, accepting the instructions. Dread washed over Maria; if even Tristan was agreeing to this terrible plan, there really was absolutely no other way.

Morgana shoved Avery in their direction, towards the somber Moz. "Thank you, Ransom. You can let the girl go after we have left. I have no real use for a dead witch right now if I have the Knight."

Avery stepped towards them, her chin tilted down and looking up at them through her dark eyelashes with a twisted grin. As she floated past Moz, he said something to the demon in a voice too quiet for Maria to hear. The possessed Avery stopped and turned to face him. Though she laughed, she did not answer him before she melted into the group. Shank and Tristan shrank away to avoid the reach of her blackened fingertips.

Returned to his feline form, Aegis circled the group with a swishing tail to assess whoever this Ransom demon was, Maria wondered if he was speaking to Jack or Ina, maybe Mori.

"Now that was a peaceful transaction, was it not?" Morgana called. "It's been pleasure doing business with you, insolent cockroaches."

The Legion officers that flanked Morgana grabbed Moz by both elbows as soon as he was within reach, pulling him away. He didn't even put up a fight; his easily earned submission broke Maria's heart.

After they had gone, the demonic blight vanished from Avery's skin even quicker than it had appeared. Black smoke trickled off her shoulders as she heaved for air.

"Why... did you let him do that?"

Her movement was slow as she fumbled for her sword, her body swaying as she was still disoriented. Avery brought the blade to her palm, missing it entirely and failing to draw blood.

"It was more important that we…. kept him away from her… than it was to keep me alive."

Then the rage ignited in her eyes as though the events were finally registering in her brain. Maria jumped forward and tried to grab Avery's shoulder before she began to run, but ended up with only a handful of her hair that slipped through her fingers before she could close them.

Kurosaki was the first to chase after her, fumbling with Moz's sword in his hands. He was promptly passed by Ina as the wolf disappeared into the woods much faster than he could.

"Lily, don't! We don't know what she's going to do!" Maria pleaded as Lily was next to follow, but she received no answer. Avery could accidentally kill her best friend in her rage; Lily was still very much human.

Tristan grabbed Lily by the arm as she tried to sprint past him, jerking her suddenly with the stop. She screamed in frustration, trying to break out of the grip of his large hand.

"I reckon she needs to cool down," he spoke calmly, no doubt trying to change the panicked atmosphere as best as he could. "She will come back;

there's no way at all she'd just leave y'behind. None of us are going to be left behind, not you an' not Moz."

Lily's defensive stance loosened as she gave up on wriggling out of Tristan's grip, either out of defeat or understanding. She looked over in Maria's direction as though she might confirm his gesture and she was suddenly aware of the burning tears collecting in her lashes.

"We'll wait then," Lily finally spoke. "If Kurosaki doesn't bring her back in a half-hour, I'll go find her myself."

— ꝭ —

Avery thundered through the trees, her rage flowing in bursts of screams and a constant pounding of her boots on the forest floor. She scanned the trees desperately for the white horse, looking for Moz. How was she going to catch up to them?

She had seen everything, lying just beneath the surface of the demon that had stolen control of her body. Avery saw the exchange through her own eyes, but as someone else watching from behind a screen.

Did Moz always feel that way? The hard look on his face when the demon spoke to him burned in her brain; the clear hatred in his eyes could have easily been meant for her. She stepped by him so closely that Avery had swelled with the hope that she could reach out and scream for help. But Moz heard nothing.

"Where... is your stupid fucking hair...," her rage turned into tears as she began to slow down.

There was nothing around her but trees. Ina's black form darted in the underbrush just far enough to stay out of Avery's way before circling in front of her to cut off Avery's raging path.

Twigs snapped behind her as a second pair of feet approached her. Defeat buckled her knees and she stopped to regain her balance. Ina circled to block her path forward, approaching Avery slowly as she sank to the forest floor.

"Did you hear what he said to the demon?"

It was Kurosaki who had followed her. Avery didn't bother wiping her face before she turned around to face him. Her eyes fell on his right hand where he held Moz's blessed sword and she froze. Wherever he was taken, he had known he was going to be helpless there.

"I can't... what are you talking about?"

"When we made the exch-I mean, when you walked back over, Moz said something to the demon. Did you hear it?"

"No, I didn't hear it at all," Avery lied.

Kurosaki tilted his head away, his mouth slightly open and forming inaudible words as he spoke his thoughts to himself. She leaned closer, hoping he would take it as a signal to let her in on his line of thoughts a little bit louder.

Instead he said, "We should probably give that Keeper of the Crossroads a ring."

— ☙ —

An air of rage was heavy around Avery when she emerged from the trees, her stride quick and determined. Lily couldn't ever recall a time she had seen such fury on the face of her best friend; she was almost sure her fist would punch a hole through the pocket of her pants as she fished around in it angrily.

"Balthazar better fuckin' know where he is," Avery's voice was lined thick with frustrated disgust.

Avery pulled out copper coins and exhaled as though finding them was a significant relief. Lily looked at Maria next to her, hoping for an explanation. She met her dark eyes and Maria flushed red.

"An offering. To summon him," she stammered with embarrassment. Lily made an attempt to smile reassuringly and Maria averted her gaze. Avery set the coins on the ground and stepped backwards before yelling up to the sky.

"Alright, I got your damned spell book!"

Lily looked around; there was no response.

"We have Mona's book," she yelled louder. "We helped you, now you have to help Moz!"

"I really do not like how you think you have me on a leash," the smoke-thick voice spoke and everyone whirled to face the wiry body emerging from the fog settling on the forest floor. "I don't *have* to help anyone."

Lily nervously twisted her grip on her bow. She could already feel this interaction going sour.

"You're forgetting that we have your wife's spell book," Avery's tone was biting, as though she had nothing to fear from the demon. "And I don't think you'll get it back until Moz is safe with us."

Balthazar's lip twitched and Lily reached behind her shoulder for an arrow, but he erupted only in laughter. The twisted cackling crescendoed as he bent backwards at the waist, laughing with his whole body.

"Avery Porter! Are you really trying to barter with a demon?"

His spine was bent too far backwards and it slowly straightened as he ended his laughing fit long enough to speak. Even Avery looked taken aback by his reaction. She shrunk into herself, her bravado visibly fading as her shoulders sank slowly.

"I don't have a choice," she said softly.

"Well, I'm not getting him. I will, however, tell you where you can find him. What you will find there should be punishment enough for trying to barter with me."

"We'll do anythin'," Tristan jumped in before Avery could answer and screw up the conversation any further.

Balthazar smiled a wide and toothy grin, no doubt satisfied by the desperation heard in Tristan's voice. When people were desperate, they made deals.

"There is a prison not far from the Brightloch walls. Normally it is used for the somewhat deserving criminals in the capitol; that is where he is being kept," he said. "Three days from here on foot."

Avery didn't even bother to politely end the conversation before looking ahead and trudging past him in their original direction. Balthazar looked back at her over his shoulder and chuckled.

"Someone's in a hurry. And rightfully so, I doubt they'll be kind to him."

Lily gave Balthazar one more cautious glance before she jogged to catch up to Avery, the band of Reapers following.

She did not know what compelled her to look behind her at the demon who still stood right where they had left him; Balthazar's tall form blending in with the trees as they put more distance between them. He watched them leave, a blood-chilling grin spread across his face.

There was a loud crack and papery rustle, Lily whirled around in fright. Avery had stopped her raged stomping with her sword held before her as she looked down at the snapped tree branch that fell only feet from where she stood.

"What the… fuck was that?"

Lily felt her heartbeat pound even in her throat as she tried to think of a way to explain how she ripped a branch from a tree.

"Avery, I did something."

The arm that held Hemlock went slack and Avery turned to look at her. Avery's skeptical raise of a thick eyebrow very easily could have challenged that the deal with Balthazar wasn't true; that Lily couldn't possibly have done anything wrong. She looked again down at the limb before turning a dismayed face to Lily.

"No, Lily, tell me you didn't," Avery begged. Lily didn't have to explain; she already knew.

"I had to. I didn't know what was happening to you down there."

The sadness in Avery's face seemed much too intense for it to be simply about the deal Lily made with Balthazar.

"I never meant for you to get sucked into this," Avery said. "You were supposed to still be at home, you have a family. Can you imagine the grief your brother is feeling right now? Did you even tell Byron you were leaving?"

"You're right," Lily answered quietly. "Which is why I did what I had to so that I make it back. So that both of us make it back. It's your family, too."

Avery pursed her lips, her sadness giving way to a look of determination that Lily felt was at least mildly assuring. "We'll make it back. I promise."

Lily nodded, accepting her answer. She tried to return the assurance to her friend, holding a hand out and cupping it gently on Avery's shoulder.

"Let's go get Moz."

CHAPTER SEVEN
BALLAD FOR AN EXORCIST

I s it just my imagination, or have we picked up some new travel buddies?"

Avery stopped and looked about their group, confused by Alice's observation as she didn't notice anyone that had not been travelling with them for the past two days. *Me, Lily, Maria, Shank, Tristan, Alice, Kurosaki... who is she talking about, then?* She turned back at Alice, her eyebrows furrowed as she turned to give Avery a perplexed shake of the head.

Alice shook her head, the action mirrored back to Avery with a sharp impatience and pointed towards the fern just before her feet. Avery's stare followed the direction Alice pointed in and saw nothing immediately of interest. Instead of shooting off a sarcastic remark to Alice, Avery crouched down to get a closer look.

Beneath the leafy comb, Avery found two black orbs bobbing about. One floated away and up the nearby trunk of a tree, its friend circling around Avery's boot.

"*Blood, blood, blood, blood, blood, blood,*" the fledgling demon squeaked.

She had almost forgotten about their nonsensical words; her days since Ardua were beginning to melt together in a jumbled lifetime. Looking back up at her friends, she saw Maria's face was alight with excitement.

"This probably means there's a town nearby! Maybe even an altar! Right, Tristan?"

The exorcist nodded, not seeming nearly as excited as the Reaper.

"Can't be sure in which direction, I'm afraid. I reckon we should keep on our path and hope they grow in number... maybe that'll point us the right way."

"*Sounds like he's saying to just ignore it,*" Aegis purred from in front of her as she stood up. "*Though I must admit, for obvious reasons I'm not terribly thrilled at the idea of more of you having demon-slaying weapons. I'll keep to your good side.*"

"We can do that," Avery said to Tristan, her exhaustion beginning to drag and lessen her voice.

The further on they walked, the more the floating orbs made their presence known. It wasn't long before their mumbling became a constant hum floating down from where they had begun to congregate in the treetops. When the Reapers would approach them, they bobbed down from their perches and out of their hiding places of the brush to inspect them; looking for feelings of misery and fear to feed upon. Avery held herself with a tight posture, making sure she was giving them no entry to prey upon her through. She couldn't let what Moz had done for them be for nothing.

A subtle snap came from somewhere around them, and Avery froze to look down at the ground below her feet. It was not her who had broken a branch, for they were all standing on a soft bed of moss. She turned slowly and found that the rest of her group was standing alert as well, swords and bows and guns pointing in every direction.

"I have a bad feeling about this all of a sudden," Kurosaki muttered.

Tristan was nodding as his gaze was slowly scanning the trees. "I reckon this is an awful lot like the situation in Ardua where Ave nearly had her face clawed off."

Avery froze with wide eyes, remembering the possessed man hanging lifelessly from the clawed creature - she had been completely covered in its blood. She watched the bobbing orbs cautiously, shifting on her heels in case she had to shy away from one of them. The demon fledglings were obviously gathering in this area, but why? How likely was it that one of them had found a soul to prey off out in the middle of nowhere?

"A... what... what the sweet fuck is that?"

Avery followed Lily's pointed finger to see the tall shape standing nearly beyond her visual capabilities as its narrow frame fit so perfectly with the slender alders. It could have been an ordinary person had it not been for its unnatural height and what looked to be long arms draping down to its knees.

Maria reached out, gently pushing Lily's arm down.

"Shh, shh. Keep quiet," she spoke softly, though Avery had a feeling Maria was just as afraid. "If we stay quiet and keep calm, there's a chance it won't even see us."

"Lower your bows," Kurosaki was whispering too, pointing his handgun down at the ground. "Step back until you're sure we're out of sight. Don't take your eyes off it. Tristan, you ready yourself in case this goes to the wind."

Avery stepped backwards slowly and her feet were wary of even the ground beneath her. With Hemlock in her right hand, she reached out to grab Lily's while keeping her eyes fixed on the eerie figure. Lily's fingers welcomed hers with a hard squeeze, not seeming to care at the moment about crushing Avery's knuckles. As they stepped backwards only the sound of their breath mixed with the quiet crunch of the earth under their boots.

The gray figure appeared to be looking about as its body swayed like faded ribbons in the wind. Avery couldn't make out where its eyes should have been. She glanced down at Aegis, who still crouched low in the ferns to watch the demon-beast in the distance. He kept quiet; perhaps the predator demon would notice them if he spoke to Avery.

Lily's fingers broke out of hers and Avery threw her gaze forward to find that the spindly beast was crouched low in a run in their direction.

"Tristan, now! Give me an in!"

Instead of drawing his handguns, Kurosaki unsheathed Moz's blessed sword and pushed to the front of the group to stand with his feet planted firmly. The demon let out a horrifying screech as flesh on the featureless head parted to reveal a mouth full of jagged teeth, salivating as it hurtled toward Kurosaki.

"Maria, Shank, get Lily out of here and back us up," Tristan said as he uncorked a large bottle he held in his giant grip.

Maria did not need to be told twice - she grabbed Lily's arm and scurried down the hill behind them again with Shank in tow. Shank moved backwards with the slope of the land and their arrow at the ready as they stood between the two women and the beast.

Not wasting any more time, Avery slit her scarred-raw palm with Hemlock and let herself stand in the veil between the living and dead as the revenants seeped up from the ground. She knew still that they would likely hesitate to attack the demon, but it surely was better than not at all.

The beast leaped upon them with sinewy muscles roping under thin, grey flesh as it lunged out of Kurosaki's quick flash of metal. Alice fled from her stance beside Avery and her pale hands wielded her short blades rather than her guns.

"Avery, Kuro, keep it busy! I'll protect Tristan!"

A vibrating screech split the air when the creature lunged for Kurosaki and caught the edge of the blade. Blood spurted, but the terrible beast was not gravely injured nor dead. The shadows in Avery's visions bobbed, unsure of what to do. Somehow Kurosaki seemed to sense her hesitation.

"Keep its back exposed, keep turning it around for Tristan," he called out as she saw Alice inching in front of Tristan towards the beast.

The exorcist was watching with an eager but analytical stare, ready to dump the contents of his bottle upon the demon. Avery had to admit she was curious to see what this potion would do. Her desire to keep Tristan and the others safe was far more overwhelming than the simple curiosity; she turned Hemlock in her fingers and gripped it tight in her oozing palm.

And to her spirits Avery commanded, "Kill it."

There was nothing in the vicinity for the spirits to turn into flying projectiles, the ferns at their feet were far too limp to cause any real damage and Avery doubted that the angry revenants could uproot an entire tree - or aim accurately enough to miss hitting Avery if they proved capable of swinging one around like a giant club.

Ghostly fingers slashed like claws upon the demon's flesh, the beast whirling around as though it was trying to find a single source. The teeth dripped with saliva when it turned in Avery's direction and her blood froze. Swatting with mile-long arms, the beast pushed through the cutting claws of Hemlock's spirits towards her.

"Good, Avery! Keep it disoriented!"

The beast cocked its head in the other direction towards where Kurosaki had called out from just as he was running towards the demon with Moz's sword held high. His voice wasn't jarring enough, as the demon stretched out an arm of sagging grey flesh like that of the elslith. Long fingers gripped Kurosaki around the shoulder and his eyes went wide with startle as they snaked toward his throat.

Avery jumped forward, bringing the heavy weight of Hemlock's blade down on the exposed limb. The demon reeled backwards, screaming in a pitch that could startle even the denizens of Od as black ooze dripped down its thin-skinned flank. She grabbed Kurosaki by the back of his black parka and pulled him backwards away from the beast to put a safe distance between them as he recovered from the scare.

Avery found herself thankful that Moz was right when he said though she didn't have a blessed sword, Hemlock's connection to Od made it possible to injure the demon-beasts.

Alice and Kurosaki crept up from behind as the creature was screeching from the pain of both the bleeding stump and the assault of revenants upon its flesh. They moved without a sound - or any sound loud enough for Avery to hear over the commotion - and Tristan raised the bottle up above his head to bring it down upon the beast. Though the demon's skull was well above even Tristan's massive frame, he reached in a bounding leap.

Glass shattered on the misshapen skull and blue fluid dripped down the translucent flesh. The terrible screeching stopped and the demon froze as though it knew exactly what was about to become of it.

Black spots began to appear on the grey sheet of skin and turned to pinpricks glowing a dull red before spitting a quick flame. The small spots of fire did not last long before the skin fell away in flurries of ashes. With no cries or screams, the demon fell towards Avery and Kurosaki onto its knees and she had an unhindered view of the beast's flesh falling away in glowing embers.

The burning body crumpled onto the side that still had a freakishly long arm and the flesh that had not yet burned away began to collapse into where the skeletal system should have resided. Avery saw that it was not a skeleton at all, but more flesh nestled deeper within the demon's body.

"Look," Alice whispered in macabre wonder with a finger pointing down at the whole other body revealed in the decay.

The man's face came into view first. His skin belonged to someone who was more than halfway through life; laugh-lines and worry wrinkles folding his freckled face. The sparse eyebrows above his closed eyes were the same moonlight grey as the hair cut close to his scalp. The last of the demon's shell burned away and revealed that his arms were folded across his chest with both hands held pointed up towards his chin and his fingers splayed as though someone had intentionally sculpted him with hands poised as the curled legs of a lifeless spider.

His shirt was an ordinary brown cotton, the brick-red trousers on his short legs equally unremarkable. He looked like anyone Avery could have seen on the streets of Centralia; what had happened to this man to make him turn into such a terrible beast?

"Poor man," Tristan murmured with pity as the sounds of the archers' feet returned to them.

Lily gripped Avery's elbow to spin her around, staring intently at her pupils in a spontaneous exam; she did so every time Avery so much as gently bumped her head back home. Her focus then shifted to the corpse that they had gathered around, her full lips parting as though she wanted to offer some form of condolence but had none that could break through the shock.

"We have to bury him," Shank finally broke the silence. "We don't know what happened to cause his possession, but I know that's what I would want."

Everyone looked to Tristan, knowing that he was an expert on burial rites or at least the closest they had to having one. He began rolling up the sleeves of his rust-splattered tunic.

"Start digging the grave."

Morgana stepped with brisk purpose down the damp hall of stone and acknowledged her officers with only the most subtle of nods. She passed many doors as she went deeper and deeper into the prison, down into the mountain's side. The specific cell she was looking for was the very last door on the right. At this depth, those incarcerated long enough may have been beginning to think that the sun was a mere rumor.

The armed soldier standing dutifully outside of the door saluted Morgana with expected reverence and she let him hold the position a little longer than she should have out of sheer pleasure that she was able to make him do so.

"At ease."

He relaxed and looked from the fixed point ahead of him to her and the metal cup of water she held in her hand.

"No charm this time, Chief?"

Morgana shook her head. "Not this time, Kryloff. We give it to him straight. Let me in."

He skipped acknowledgement of her order and instead turned immediately to unlock the iron padlock on the door. With a clank of old metal, the door opened and the light from the hallway was swallowed by a cell of pitch-darkness.

Morgana sucked in a breath, knowing that the cell was rank with the smell of piss. She stepped in cautiously over the door frame as her eyes began to adjust in the darkness.

The crumpled form that was William Mosley was right where she had left him; miserable and pinned to the wall in iron chains. She didn't hear even the smallest mutter from him in the long time she stood there; was he dead? Of course not, not as long as the Knight was still there.

Would she be able to convince him to give away the location of the last Knight? Her life, Sera's life, and whether she ever saw her husband again counted on him doing so. Too much was at stake for her to be gentle, Morgana knew she would have to use her heaviest leverage if she was ever going to get what she wanted from the Beldam.

She grinned when she remembered exactly how she gained her biggest advantage in this round of cat and mouse: her knowledge. William sacrificed himself, something she thought the man was too selfish to be capable of, for only one person.

"Tell me where the Knight of Spirit is and maybe I'll decide not to gut Avery Porter. No, maybe I'll decide she gets a swifter death. Don't you think she'd appreciate that, William? It's up to you."

Her voice was soft, but her words were as sharp as coffin nails when she ducked down lower to let the light from the hall illuminate his bruised and battered face.

"You... you leave her alone," blood sputtered from William's lips and Morgana couldn't help but lean backwards with a cackling laugh.

"I'm so glad I found the gap in your armor, William. I mean, that the Berserker Witch was the one who happened to go to Od? It was goddamn luck that Ransom snatched her up and I found out what is at stake here for you. It's her."

She kicked the tin cup to the wall. William winced as precious water splashed and began to seep into the cracked surface of the stone floor.

"Act careless, don't give away what the gap in your *armor is."*

She frowned, hoping that his Knight didn't overhear hers. Morgana stood with her hands on her hips as she looked down at him, shaking her head.

"Pathetic. It really is fucking pathetic."

Morgana crouched down again, looking him in his bloodied face and he scowled.

"Brother. Tell me where the last Knight is and if you are true to your word, you will be a free man once again."

"Then I'll rot."

He spat a glob of blood onto her boots and she stood up. Morgana grimaced before kicking him swiftly in the ribs and he tipped over as far as the chains would let him. His cries of pain echoed in the cramped space. Morgana began to leave but stopped in the open doorway of the prison cell, looking back at him one more time. Seeing a fearsome Knight cry with such agony? Shameful. He had no idea what pain really was.

"That can be arranged, I assure you. The maggots will feast like kings and you will *still* be unworthy."

She slammed the door behind her and stared at the opposite wall as she sucked in a deep breath in a pitiful attempt to calm her temper. By the time her shoulders finished sinking with the exhale, she already tore off her heeled boot and threw it violently at the wall.

"Son of a fucking bitch!" She wanted to scream, but it came out in a dry hiss; she did not want Mosley to hear her and gain the satisfaction of her frustration.

"Chief?"

Instead of answering Kryloff, she put her hands on her hips and sucked in another breath before she stooped down to retrieve her boot.

"No more glamour spells. No more tricks. No more asking nicely," she said with as calm of a voice as her fiery temper would allow. "We take no defensive stance and let them come to us, Peter will give Mosley one last chance before we gut everyone who means a sliver of anything to him. No holding back, he'll have to give up the Knight then. From here, he can only go to Brightloch or Eyon. I'll be watching. We'll smoke him out and see where he goes if he tries to lie his way out."

— 🐦 —

"Thank the gods!" Tristan cried out joyously as he hurried towards the cluster of thatched-roof buildings visible through the trees and just over the next ledge.

He slowed just before approaching the small village when he noticed an unsettling lack of movement. Above the murmurs of his friends as they caught up to him, he heard the squawking of crows. The presence of so many scavenging birds in a small village? Something was wrong.

Tristan stopped, unsure if he had the strength to see what had unfolded in the small community. Alice stopped beside him, putting a gentle hand on his arm.

"We don't have to go in there. I think we know what happened here," she whispered and he knew that his concern was justified when she mirrored it. He looked down at her, but Alice was watching the flock of corvids with her golden eyes narrowed; he hated how refined her intuition was at terrible times.

He shook his head. "No, we have to."

Tristan shrugged out of her reach, the tread of his footsteps solemn and heavy as he stepped towards the silent village. It was then that the stench began to curl around his nose, reaching his friends behind him as well, for he heard one of them retch.

Masses of crimson and torn flesh became clearer when he stood between the first two homes of tied branches, the corvids that perched upon them paid Tristan no mind; his horror was locked on the sight of mass gore. Tears rolled down his cheeks as he gazed upon what was left of the town, what the demon had done to them. What the Beldam had done to them.

He broke out of his frozen terror and cried out angrily, swinging his sword at the birds to frighten them away from the bodies. With a loud flap of wings, they fled only to land two roofs away. They watched him with beady black eyes as his own cried, his nose dripping but he was far too angry to care.

"Oh gods, what have they done," Lily was the only one who spoke.

He saw in his peripheral vision that her bow was hanging on her shoulder as both of her hands covered her mouth in shock. She buckled forward at the knees, as did he.

"We can't bury every single one of them," he cried, his hands on his knees as he bent forward. "We... we just can't."

Burying the possessed man had exhausted all of them in both the emotional and physical senses, but for all these innocent people? They deserved the rite, he had no doubt about that; but he didn't think he had it in him to do it. Not when he suspected there were children amongst the corpses. Images of his daughter flashed in his mind, flickers of her golden eyes and bouncy blonde curls. She was gone forever and so were they.

Tristan wiped off his face with the back of his sleeve, doing whatever he could to regain his ability to face his friends again. When he turned, he saw Avery standing with wide eyes. Her head flicked fast in many directions, her grip on the sword of necromancy twisting with unrest. What did she see?

"Ave... Ave, what's tha' matter?"

"They're... gods, what horrible thing!" Avery stammered to get the words out as she fumbled for the looking glass around her neck. She yanked it off from around her neck, thrusting the foul thing into Tristan's hands. He was confused at first as to what he was supposed to do with the glass until he remembered Avery holding it up to her eye after encountering Balthazar in the graveyard. When he did the same, his stomach twisted.

The spirits were standing still, like eerie pillars of shadow above their mangled bodies. As Tristan watched them, they watched him back with eyes of black. *Good gods* - was this what Avery saw on a daily basis?

What did it mean if their spirits were here, not with the gods and not in Od? Was the line of death already blurring by the hand of Beldam? Nothing in his studies could have prepared Tristan for this.

Tristan lowered the glass and now it was only the corpses he saw. He gently draped the necklace back around Avery's head and onto her neck, marveling at her ability to keep as much sanity as she had while seeing the terrible sight that rattled him.

"We're too late… but we need to search the town. I reckon if we're lucky, they'll have an altar to Onja."

"I wouldn't say victory was with these people," Kurosaki said darkly, turning his head over his shoulder either to muffle his remark or to begin searching. Tristan was still far too stunned to chide the young man; he felt shameful to admit there was a chance they could benefit from the town when its occupants were all dead.

"C'mon, Aegis. Let's look," Avery spoke in a low voice. The cat crept ahead of her as Avery passed Tristan, the collar of her black shirt pulled over her nose to block out the stench of rot.

Tristan watched the swishing tail as they navigated through the cadavers and he found himself still, contempt freezing his every sinew of muscle. Avery's head dipped to look at the bodies, the torn people she passed. He didn't have to see her face to know her terror. All the while, the demon made no such motion, treading with his Reaper. Business as usual.

Hatred bubbled in his heart. It was Aegis' kind that had committed an unprovoked atrocity. What made the familiars assigned to Reapers so different than the terrible beasts? *Cute and fuzzy vessels and not much else.*

He stopped his hateful inner monologue to remember the bobbing black orbs all around them. Tristan immediately put himself back into check, cracking his neck and straightening his spine as he imagining the negative sludge rolling off him in waves. To lose his calmness would have meant to lose his only defense against the demon fledglings.

Consecrate my sword and I reckon I'll be the bastard who comes out on top!

Tristan stood upright, still swaying on his heels with dizzying disbelief. He still had to see if there was an altar to Onja; he had to make sure that what had happened to this town would not happen to Centralia or Brightloch.

As he walked in a daze with his sword held low and nearly dragging on the ground, he passed homes with their doors wide open. He saw unmoving feet in view from the gaping entryways, heard the buzzing of flies, and vomited. The demon from the woods had taken lives so quickly that none of these people had enough time to flee. He wiped the bile away from his lips with a cloth from his rucksack.

"There's a couple of shrines, over here!"

Tristan hurried excitedly towards the edge of the village to follow Alice's voice. Turning a corner, he saw the lilac-haired woman waving everyone else over. Before her stood twin stone altars.

When he got closer, he saw the markings on the obelisks. One sarsen point held a carved relief depicting a tree, half of its branches lush with leaves while its opposite side was bare. At the foot of the obelisk was a stone cauldron settled into the earth, but he knew he would not be making a sacrifice to this vessel.

"This one is for Malo," he knew he should have felt ashamed of the frustration in his voice but turned to examine the other instead.

His face lit up in relief when he saw the etched broadsword and shield etched into the obelisk; the shield bore the sigil of five circles connected by intercrossing lines, belonging to Onja.

"It's... Her," he whispered breathlessly.

"I'll start the f-" Shank began to offer and Tristan cut them off.

"I appreciate yer offer, but I need to be the one to do this. To ensure we do all the motions the right way."

He approached the fire pit, knowing he did not need any kind of wood or kindling. Striking a match, he dropped it into the pit and it erupted into a healthy flame that hovered just above the bottom of the stone pit. His friends stared at the flame in enchantment while he was focused solely on his duty.

"Empty yer bags! You offer up a sacrifice an' make it your most treasured item on your person."

Tristan then knelt before the stone cauldron, taking every jar of moon-blessed water he had in his possession and dumped them into the basin. He bowed low, pressing his forehead into the dirt as a sensation both sublime and familiar came over him: the gods were listening.

He got back up to his feet to find Alice and Kurosaki frantically dumping the clips of their guns, presumably wanting to bless each one of the bullets. The act seemed almost greedy, but he could not fault them. Alice turned a small bottle over in her hand, and if he recalled correctly it contained a liquor; a sacrifice that bore no significant meaning to Alice as far as he knew, but would likely suffice. Beside her, Kurosaki looked down at a tooth held in his open palm.

Though his familiar had not been around since Kurosaki was Saved the previous year, Tristan still knew well of their friendship and what giving up an artifact of the familiar's host body meant to him. Onja would bless him well for the raccoon tooth.

Tristan turned to watch Avery next to him, curious as to what she was rummaging through her rucksack for.

"Pants?"

She didn't react to his bafflement and he felt a pang of guilt when she looked at them with longing. He then realized that they were the last thing in her possession from her life in Ardua; the life he and Moz had stolen from her.

His friends all held their beloved possessions: Maria's necklace, Shank's scrimshaw knife, a drawing scribbled by Lily's nephew. They then looked at him as though they already knew what he was about to place down.

Tears burned in his eyes, knowing exactly what the precious item he was about to part with. Tristan looked down at his hand, using his right thumb and index finger to wriggle the gold ring free. He needed the gods and all their might, everything he could get if he was going to save Moz and the friends who counted on him.

"I'm so sorry, Helena," he whispered through biting tears as he held the gold band in his open palm. He knew his departed wife would forgive him whenever he saw her again.

Tristan wiped his eyes, exhaling loudly and turning back towards the group.

"We each throw our items into the fire and place our weapons into the water to be blessed," he instructed.

They looked at him as though he had just given them the most bizarre set of instructions and none of them even inched toward the hot lick of the flames.

Avery balled up the pants in her fist, throwing it hard at the holy flame as though it would ensure her sacrifice was received. Sparks scattered into the dirt and disappeared before the denim was swallowed by fire. She looked at Tristan as though unsure of what to do next. He waved her over.

She unsheathed Hemlock, gently lowering it into the waters of the cauldron. He reeled back in surprise when the eye of the hilt opened and looked about the inside of the cauldron. Would a weapon crafted by the

Beldam be unable to receive Onja's blessing? Tristan hoped for Avery's sake that it could.

"Wait!"

Avery leaned forward, shoving her hand into the water and dropping a dagger. Tristan's eyes widened when he saw Moz's small blade, the dagger he had given to her when they had fled Ardua. He looked at her and the way she stared at the knife with a blank expression.

Tristan gently put a hand on her shoulder and Avery looked at him in surprise.

"He's gonna be okay. Don't y'worry."

Tristan performed the ritual for each of his friends. Alice and Kurosaki dumped in all their guns and clips, getting flustered when both of their piles reached above the surface of the water. Maria, Shank, and Lily dropped in the entire contents of their quivers; each looking a little wary of the fact that they would have to distinguish which arrows belonged to whom when the ritual was over.

His stomach clenched up when it came time for him to make his sacrifice. Tristan approached the fire, holding his wedding band in his shaking hand. He couldn't hold back this time from sobbing, too sorrowful to be ashamed. After a long hesitation, he kissed the wedding ring.

"Please... please help us," he pleaded before tossing it into the fire.

He watched the licking flames swallow the last item he had from his wife. Gone. Tristan couldn't bring himself to move.

A small hand slid into his and he looked down at Alice.

"You're almost there," she spoke gently. "You're strong."

He nodded, knowing that there was no point in stopping. Tristan stepped to the cauldron, unsheathing his humble sword and dropping it into the water. He closed his eyes.

"May your victory smile upon all your children and all your kindred, Queen Onja. Hear our prayer, Lady of Battles Won. Reward our strife, judge with mercy, and act with justice."

With a crackling whoosh, the flame vanished and the woods fell into silence. He looked up, watching the white ashes as they were picked up by a faint wind before the ash disappeared into the treetops. He picked up the

dripping sword and wiped it tenderly with his sleeve before sheathing it again. Tristan again fell to his knees at the foot of the cauldron.

"It is done."

"How will we know if it worked?" Maria began plucking her arrows out of the water, making sure she grabbed only the ones with the green bands and golden feathers.

"I reckon the only way is to slay those demon - pardon my language - bastards."

Tristan turned and trudged back into the site of the massacre. As his friends still distributed and returned the blessed weapons, he locked his eyes on one of the demon fledglings bobbing past the hut nearest him. The orb bobbed carelessly towards the center of the town even though there were no souls left to latch onto.

He approached it from behind and wrought the edge of his sword down. The orb solidified under the metal only as the exorcist split it in two. Black ooze leaked from the split and the Leech fell to the dirt.

"*Bl... bl...*" the Leech's nonsensical chirping faded to silence.

Tristan had slain the demon fledgling with his sword with the same ease as Moz. He looked up and behind him, hoping that at least one of his friends had witnessed. He found Avery staring at the dead Leech with wide eyes. Her gaze shifted up to Tristan and her small mouth spread into a grin.

"I reckon you'll forgive me again... feck yeah!"

— 🦇 —

They put the altar and shambles of the ruined town far behind them; the joy from their consecrated weapons was again tarnished by the bodies they had to step over to get them in their holy state. Avery led the group in a reckless daze, stumbling over the broken terrain.

She looked down at the dagger she still gripped in her hand, dry of the last holy droplets. The brown leather grip felt smooth in her hand in comparison to the ragged wrap around Hemlock and she found herself turning it around in her fingers, fidgeting to soothe her nerves.

"Be honest. Losing Moz hurt you more than it hurt the others, didn't it," Lily whispered over Avery's shoulder, her sudden approach lacked caution or warning but it failed to startle Avery in her thick head fog.

Avery looked at her friend, unsure of what she should say. Was it true? Moz was closer to all the other Reapers and it would have made sense if they were struck with an even greater grief. But when she thought of the buzzing in her heart when he had first hugged her and the warmth of his kiss when it had happened, she knew that it wasn't grief at all that she felt; it was a hunger for vengeance.

Grief was something felt when someone had died and she knew with burning certainty that Moz had not. The notion seemed impossible to Avery after all the brilliant flashes of sword steel and the pure drive to see the end of the Knights. It was not at all a possibility, not when there was so much still to be done.

"It's getting late," Avery spoke to everyone else, ignoring Lily. "We stop here for the night."

No one argued or offered any reason why they should keep going. Alice and Kurosaki threw down their sacks, collapsing into the dirt next to them. Everyone prepared their own part of the circular encampment, sticking close together in the spot of the forest they had halted in. Avery slunk away, sliding downhill to be just out of earshot before sitting down against an alder tree.

It didn't take long for the crunch of footsteps to follow and for Lily's quiver to appear next to her. She sat down next to Avery, seeming to know not to say anything immediately and they lingered in a comfortable silence- before Lily began running her mouth.

"Maria is hurt, too," Lily continued their earlier conversation, leaning back on her hands as she spoke. "He's her best friend and the difference in the way she is processing makes it all the more obvious.

Is it my unfortunate duty to point out the very obvious and fucked-up situation that is having a soft spot for the person who abducted you? Yes. I mean, bloody hell, Avery Noelle Porter. You can't make up shit like that! But do I think that's what your relationship remains grounded in? No, I don't. Though circumstances started out in the worst way possible, it's clear that you're still here because of mutual trust and care. You're still here because you want to be and he is kind because he realizes he put you in a bad situation and sees all the good things about you."

Avery felt Lily's eyes on her, but couldn't bring herself to meet her look and instead focused into the thick of the forest. Her eyes were heavy with sleep deprivation and gazing into the vast optic field of green felt like the closest she would get to any rest.

"I think in a way," Avery finally whispered "I wish I was like him. I'd give anything to be brave. This whole time I've been so afraid about what's going to happen to them, to you, to the world, and selfish as it is, to me. But he was never shaken."

Lily paused in thought before speaking. "I don't think bravery is the absence of fear. I think it's knowing how afraid you are and doing it anyway."

That didn't make any sense at all to Avery; she knew what bravery was and this wasn't it. She said nothing to Lily, not wanting to spark any kind of a philosophical argument.

"I've been avoiding asking you," Lily said instead "and the others are too afraid to ask. What did he say to you out there? When you know, you were...."

Avery had pushed the words out of her brain, put them in a box for her to open and deal with its contents at another time. But now here was the person who mattered most to her, asking in. Avery could never say no to her, and Lily knew that.

From behind a screen of cloud she still saw the Knight clear as day. A droplet of blood began to collect on Moz's nose, as though straining the monster for the last time. His ruined brow was furrowed in anger, but his eyes were glassy with sadness.

"*Avery, I trust you. With my heart and with my life.*"

Avery repeated the words back to Lily and they felt empty in her own mouth. Her sister looked at her with her mouth agape, uncertain of what to say. Lily turned and looked ahead into the forest where Avery had buried her attention.

"Avery, I'm sorry for what I said. Just now."

The familiar heaviness of Lily's arm slid across her shoulders. Gentle and unobtrusive comfort.

"Don't worry," Lily spoke. "We'll find him."

Avery let a smile creep onto her lips with a mask of optimism; she wasn't so sure that they *would* find Moz. Not without any additional help, anyway. She stood up, gathering her cloak around her arms as she looked down at Lily.

"Let's walk back, I need to speak with Tristan."

Lily followed without asking what the matter of discussion was, falling out of Avery's trail and toward Shank's direction. Avery turned to look at the exorcist as he pulled out a woven blanket from his rucksack. She approached him, unconcerned by his startled jump when he found her standing over him.

"Fer the love of-"

"I have something to ask of you," Avery said, cutting off his surprised cry.

He raised a strawberry-blonde eyebrow, seeming suspicious already.

"And what is that?"

"In Ardua, you gave me - forcibly, mind you - an inhalant to sleep. That night I dreamt of a graveyard, the very same one we found Balthazar in the next day. I need to use it again, to see if I can find where Moz is."

"Avery, yer out of yer bloody mind!"

He erupted in rage that she had not been expecting at all and she jumped backwards in fright when his large frame suddenly shot up, fearful that he would strike her.

"I... I just thought-"

"That wasn't the work of the herbs I gave you, but of the demon who I reckon had long ago set its sights on you! Feckin' Balthazar and... Yer dabblin' with dark things, why can't y'see that?"

She opened her mouth, unsure of how else to respond besides whispering "I just want to find Moz."

Tristan's angry expression vanished and he looked down at the ground.

"I do too, Ave. But that's not the way. Moz trusted us to find him and I reckon with confidence."

"I just hope his trust hasn't been misplaced," Avery murmured and she left Tristan behind without another word as she started toward where the others were setting up camp.

Avery was restless long after her companions had drifted to sleep; her eyes were wide as she searched for the strange black shapes of the Leeches. She found nothing and yet couldn't relax. The forest was eerily still. Exhaustion overwhelmed her will to stay awake not long before the morning sky began to burn orange and purple.

Even as the Reapers were packing to resume their trek, Avery was silent as she counted all the ways that Moz was foolish to trust them.

They were nothing without a Knight; they were sitting ducks for any other Knight who came across them. Even with their consecrated demon-slaying weapons, it was no match for the titanic beasts.

Avery shared none of her concerns. She knew it wasn't the right thing to do when Lily and Maria were chattering away happily as they walked. An air of optimism surrounded the group, except for her, and so she led them to avoid any heads turning around to ask prying questions.

"Four Reapers up ahead," Aegis warned. *"Each with a familiar. I recognize none of them."*

Avery drew Hemlock, holding her fist upright to stop the group - just as she had seen Moz do so many times. Lily stopped next to her, holding her bow at ease and pointed down towards the ground. She looked at Avery inquisitively and then up their path as though there was something she had missed in the tall bushes and ferns.

"Reapers up ahead," Avery murmured.

"Jack says it's likely they've noticed us, too. I agree with the boy. Move ahead cautiously."

Avery dropped her fist and gripped Hemlock with both hands, stepping carefully forward with eyes sweeping across their surroundings. Her senses were overwhelmed as she tried to distinguish the movement of the underbrush of the forest as caused by the wind or unannounced bodies. Were these Reapers specifically looking for them or was it by mere coincidence?

"Aegis says he doesn't recognize their familiars' signatures," Avery relayed to the rest of the group. "So, at the very least, it's not Morgana."

Even knowing it wasn't any Legion members they had already come across, she still felt unsure as of what to expect. She prayed to Ara that this would be a casualty-free encounter if one couldn't be avoided altogether.

They carried forward at a more cautious pace, looking in all directions in case they should find themselves ambushed. Snapping twigs came from ahead of them, not matching their own footsteps. Once more Avery signaled the group to stop when the faint murmur of voices floated up from beyond the next dip of hill.

The grizzly bear didn't make its presence known until it stood up on its hind legs, appearing massive even with the dozens of yards between them. Much shorter human figures emerged from the fog at either side of the bear. Despite the distance, Avery saw the black auras buzzing around their heads - the mark of a Reaper.

"Oh gods," Lily muttered breathlessly from somewhere behind her at the sight of the large familiar.

"Defensive stand," Avery looked over her shoulder at her friends, Shank met her gaze first and nodded.

She turned forward. "We have to hope that they're either neutral or against the Beldam. No one makes a move unless we are explicitly threatened."

From somewhere amongst the trees came a guttural bellow, the bizarre sound chilling Avery's blood. She immediately regretted her decision to stand down but doubted that she would have stood a fighting chance against a grizzly bear anyway.

The bear dropped back down to all fours, following its Reapers as they ran towards them with heads made of buzzing black auras. Avery stood solid in place, keeping Hemlock low at her side but with twitching muscles if she were to find any reason to attack quickly.

Aegis scrambled out of the hood of her cloak and leapt off her shoulder, landing nimbly on his feet. He edged carefully through the ferns towards the incoming Reapers, pausing before he turned back to look over his haunches at Avery.

"Avery, do your best not to panic when you see it."

"The bear? It's a little late for that!"

"I was talking about the alligator, but you can pick your poison," he purred.

It was only then that she saw the squat reptile treading through the fern towards them, plowing down the flora in its path with its low-hanging belly. Though the slow speed at which it travelled wasn't menacing, she found herself quivering in fear at the sight of the beast she thought confined only to swamps and textbooks.

The Reapers passed the alligator with a much faster pace, the weapons they held were slowly lowered as they approached when Avery and the others were still not taking an aggressive stance.

When the buzzing black auras faded, Avery found they were a strange group of kids; none of them could have been a day older than eighteen nor a day shy of sixteen. The shortest girl had hair the color of pink frosting, gathered in short pigtails no longer than her jawbone. Around her forehead she wore big goggles, lenses tinted green were mounted to a wide band of brown leather. She wielded a throwing axe in each hand, red ribbons tied to the handles, a wicked grin still spread across her face.

"Ease up, Cassie," the blonde girl spoke to her shorter companion. The girl pouted and lowered her axes reluctantly.

Next to Cassie was a young boy with russet brown skin, watching Avery's group with wide eyes as though he was frightened of what the elder Reapers might do to him. Twigs were caught in his thick mess of black hair and he held his sword with flimsy uncertainty that would have made Moz fume if he had been present.

"I can tell you aren't Reapers rallying for the Knights, taking into account the three humans with you" the tallest girl with long and wild blonde hair spoke, looking at Tristan as though she was sizing up the biggest member of their group. Her gaze shifted back to Avery at their forefront.

"Two," Kurosaki corrected her as though he didn't want his status as a Saved to be overlooked.

"My name is Theirrin," she continued without acknowledging the correction. She nodded towards the weary boy and rose-haired girl. "That's Rowan and Cassie, back there is Vinny."

Avery assumed she was mentioning the boy who lingered at the back of their group. He stared back at her with pitch-dark eyes, watching her carefully with both of his swords twisting in his grip. Anger radiated from him in waves as though Avery herself was personally responsible for an unspeakable wrongdoing against the boy.

"We need to know for certain where you stand with the Beldam's decision to merge the living with Od and her Knights," Vinny spoke, his voice flat.

Avery's grip on Hemlock twisted nervously. If her answer wasn't the right one, she could end up having to kill a group of kids.

"We're doing our best to help ensure the balance," Avery carefully chose her words. "We have a friend we need to rescue... a Reaper with a Knight who has defied the Beldam."

Avery decided not to let them in on the fact that they also knew the whereabouts of the final Knight - that could be saved for when she was clear about their intentions. What were they doing out in the woods anyway?

"What do you mean defied the Beldam?" Theirrin looked at her with narrowed eyes.

"What Avery means is," Tristan cut in. "Our friend Moz has the Knight of Water, but I reckon he's kept it under tight control. He knows how he's bein' used and how it's wrong. A Knight working to kill the Knights has been a fantastic miracle."

The younger group of Reapers looked at each other, still skeptical and the boy called Rowan looked particularly terrified. Cassie looked past Avery and pointed in the direction of Maria and Shank.

"Moz... hey, I think I know that name. I think I've seen you two before."

Avery turned around and watched Maria turn her pointer finger in towards her sternum. "Who, me?"

Cassie nodded. "From Wrencrest. You two left with a man named Moz in a pair of longboats, headed west out of the swamps. Kind of a stupid and hard name to forget, right? But you're saying he was a Knight?"

Maria nodded. Avery couldn't help but wonder about how Maria and Shank left with Moz, though that was an explanation to save for another time. When Moz was there as well.

"Moz was taken by the Beldam's legion," Maria said. "Balthazar told us he's being kept in a prison just outside of Brightloch. Do you know where that is?"

She watched Theirrin and Vinny exchange concerned frowns, seeming to already know what the other was thinking about the situation.

"We do," Vinny answered. "It's a day from here. We're coming from the Reapers Outpost. Not at all where we were headed."

The what? Avery didn't have to ask for clarification, for the confusion painted on her face must have been clear enough for him to explain.

"Reapers have banded together and have a small cooperative commune northeast of Brightloch. When we hear about a demon problem, we take care of it. We're headed to Centralia. The place seems to have been completely overrun."

A pang of guilt hit her hard; these young Reapers were going to clean up the mess they had left behind.

"We can take care of all the demons quicker if we can get to our friend and end the Knights once and for all. Will you help us rescue him?"

Theirrin shook her head sadly. "No, we won't. I must take a stand, but I must protect my pack even more. We'll take you there, but we won't go inside. I promise we'll find another way to help you later - we'll try to come back this way and stay close enough for Jasper to hear your demons."

Theirrin nodded towards the bat perched on Vinny's shoulder, clinging with small claws and leathery wings spread down his arm and up his neck. Avery felt herself sink with disappointment, but she understood why Theirrin refused to drag her companions into danger. This wasn't their problem at all and Avery had to admit that she likely would have done the same thing.

"I completely get it," Avery said. "We appreciate anything you decide to do to help us, thank you."

Theirrin grinned, showing off the small gap between her two front teeth. "Let us carry on then."

The girl looked back towards the grizzly bear lurking behind the group of children and it was not until Theirrin approached it that Avery noticed a navy and gold saddle had been outfitted to it. The familiar crouched as low to the ground as it could get, allowing the girl to climb atop it and slide into the saddle.

"We're going west, Oonlok."

Cassie looked down at the stout frame of the alligator with a pout. "You sure I can't outfit you with a nice saddle, Grim? Look at how cool they look!"

The gator's throat vibrated as though to laugh, swinging around its large body awkwardly to follow the grizzly bear back into the direction they had come from. Avery looked down at Aegis with raised brows and he met her bewildered look.

"Perhaps now you'll be thankful to have me."

"I'll make sure I won't forget it."

CHAPTER EIGHT
STRENGTH

rincess, over there!"

There was no need for Mara to clarify; Yumi's head was already turning towards the other end of the hall where the revenant had snapped into sight. Owen's eyes were wide with fear as he approached Yumi with the strong stench of Od rolling off him in rank waves.

"Princess Yumi, I fear Avery is in grave danger!"

Her jaw hardened, anger tightening her every muscle and the rabbit in her arms flinched. "Danger of what? Of who?"

"She is alive and well for now, but I fear for her future. Morgana and a demon had used her as a bargaining chip to get to the Knight of Water. Avery and the other Reapers are planning a rescue, but I fear that this stand will be their last."

Before she could stop herself, her free hand flew out and closed around the collar of his shirt, pulling him forward with her dark eyes flaming with rage. Owen's eyes bulged with fear as his feet lifted off the ground and he gawked at the thick muscle of Yumi's bicep.

"Where were they before you left for Od? Where will they go to find the Knight of Water?"

The dead boy looked down at her handful of his shirt and then back up at her face, visibly fearful of her anger. He was possibly even more frightened by the realization that she could grab him, her mere touch giving him as much life and substance as she had.

"Let the little boy go, Princess. This is not his doing."

She hesitated, not yet able to calm herself. Finally, her fingers uncurled from around the fabric and she stepped back. Owen's shoulders sank with relief when his feet hit the floor again.

"Just south of a tiny commune named Damiria when I had left them. A third of the way between here and Centralia. Balthazar spoke of a prison just outside the walls where Moz is being kept. I couldn't stand by any longer and just let this happen!"

Traitor's Brig. Yumi wasted no time with a response, she was already storming towards her chamber to prepare herself for a journey to the feared prison. She strode through the west wing with fast purpose, the thick carpet muting her ungraceful stomps. Faces of royal portraits blurred past her as she found herself nearly blinded with rage, passing through a gilded foyer to fly down the southern wing.

She came upon the carved door leading to the southern tower and yanked the iron handle hard with the hand that wasn't clutching Mara to her side. Owen's meek presence trailed after her as she stomped up the spiral of marble stairs. She opened the door of her chamber just before she could find herself exhausted from the ascent, catching sight of the setting sun glistening over the Stillmaw Sea.

Yumi remembered she had asked to keep her chambers in the southern tower specifically for the sight, not knowing her chasm of isolation from the living would only grow wider with this separation from the rest of the castle.

Yumi gently set Mara on the ground before yanking open a drawer in her bureau. Inside was an assortment of corsets, each of them she tossed aside carelessly onto the floor. From the drawer beneath it, she extracted a thin iron rod and shut it. With the metal rod between two fingers, she fumbled with her other hand around the bottom of the top drawer.

"Aha," she mumbled, sliding the metal rod into a circular hole cut into the bottom of the drawer in such a way that the rod was the only thing that could conceivably fit.

Pushing upwards, a false bottom in the drawer lifted. Inside the hidden compartment were small daggers, a throwing axe, and a bottled potion that she was still not sure of the purpose it should be used for.

"Where did you get all of that? How on earth did those even fit in there?"

Yumi had nearly forgotten about Owen until he spoke up from behind her. She quickly grabbed the daggers and axe, setting them atop the bureau before bounding the room in one leap to grab her cloak from a hook.

"It's amazing what you can get away with when no one is paying attention," she said simply.

It was true; the Princess had become an article of the background in a world where people feared demon-beasts, looking to only their king and gods to save them. The royal guard even acknowledged her only if she was the only member of the royal family present. Get them in a crowded room and it wasn't hard to lift small items that they kept so ready and accessible on their person.

"That's incredibly sad," his voice was thick with sorrow and she shrugged. It was mighty beneficial to her now.

She pulled the hood of the cloak over her head, putting on a weapon belt to hold her stolen goods.

"You stay here, okay Mara?"

"What was I going to do, block your exit? I'm a rabbit."

Yumi ignored the exasperated remark and turned to Owen.

"You, on the other hand, I'll need you."

He lifted a brow, clearly unsure of her intentions.

"Why? Where are we going?"

"Outside the wall. We're going to get Avery."

— 🦇 —

Aegis awoke from his slumber to find it was still the dead of night. What was left of the campfire was now glowing coals that cast the band of Reapers in a dim, orange light. Something in the air had changed.

He stood up on all four paws, the tail of his earthly feline form swishing as he waited. The air turned with the sharp burn of sweet whiskey on his tongue and Aegis recognized the underlying scent of graveyard dirt instantly: Balthazar.

But where? And why?

Aegis looked behind him at where Avery was sleeping against a tree trunk and he debated whether he should wake her. Upon her forehead glowed a white sigil: a hexagon with lines darting in and out of its sides, an arrow slashing through the middle and pointing up towards the part in Avery's hair.

Mona's sigil!

Her eyelids opened, her orbital cavities containing the same bright light where her eyes should have been. He mewed, trying to wake anyone up as he watched Avery float upward to her feet and hovered with only the toes of her boots to the earth. None of the Reapers even stirred- *curse this form!*

He turned to wake Tristan only to find that Lily, Maria, and the young Reaper named Cassie had risen to the tips of their toes as well, glowing sigils painted on their brows and light spilled from their eye sockets.

They began to drift deeper into the trees, arms loose at their sides and dragging their toes across the ground as an invisible force pulled them.

I have to follow them!

The air went cool with the waking signature of another demon - *peppermint burning the tongue, spears of ice, cerulean streaking in the sky, the dripping marrow of bone.* Aegis turned to see Ina's head raised and her ears rigid as she watched the trees beyond the floating women.

"What is he doing here?"

Aegis took no time to propose any theories as to why Balthazar was nearby or what he was doing, but instead darted to follow the four women. He passed Oonlok and Grim as they watched passively, perhaps deciding that Aegis and Ina's actions were enough to ward off whatever was happening.

"No time, wake up Shank and come with me!" He called out behind him to Ina.

He darted to follow the girls as they were dragged towards figures slowly becoming visible in the thick fog. Instantly he recognized Balthazar's lanky form, beside him was the shorter and fuller frame of Mona; the crown of curls and gardenia upon her head taking a distinct shape. The goddess of witches was speaking in a silk-soft voice and Aegis' hearing was not quite strong enough to discern words of the non-demon.

The heavy pound of paws came upon him quickly before Ina passed him, her growls rumbling low.

"Aegis, Ina," Balthazar addressed them as they approached. His hand was held upward at waist height just at his side, drawing it back at his side upon speaking. Beside him, Mona watched with shining eyes - sublime and cautious.

The four witches floated before them, perched tall on only the tips of their toes. Ina crept in low on her haunches, growling with bared teeth as she closed in on Balthazar's flank. He regarded her only briefly, not taking her canine threats seriously. Aegis slinked around

Avery's boots to sit between them and the holy - and unholy - figure.

"What is it that you want, Balthazar?"

The Demon of the Crossroads grinned at the question, holding his hands out as though to make a display of his innocence. Aegis wasn't so quick to believe it.

"Freedom, brother Aegis. You saw how your Reaper acted as though she was in a position to control me. I simply want to remove that leverage."

"How are you going to do that?"

As though to answer his question, he raised one open hand higher to level with his sternum. Avery broke out of the line of levitating girls, her boots dragging forward and Aegis darted out of the way to avoid being crushed. He whipped around to face Balthazar, anger bubbling in his voice when he spoke.

"I know you are angry, but don't-"

He stopped when he watched Balthazar circle around Avery until he was at her back, undoing a metal buckle and reaching a slender hand into the rucksack she kept on even in her sleep. Aegis didn't want to admit even to himself the relief he felt when he realized his Reaper would not be harmed.

"We are taking back the spell book. You will have it again when you need it."

Avery had been so terrified of losing the spell book that she kept it on her person at all times, and there was Balthazar simply plucking it right out of her possession. Balthazar extracted the leather-bound tome, pausing before stepping backwards and handing it over dutifully to his wife.

Mona took the grimoire into her hands, looking down at it with wide eyes of disbelief that softened - visibly relieved that her sacred book was back in her possession. Mona looked up at the faces of her underlings, the glow of their eyes remained blank, as she clutched the spell book to her bosom. She looked past them towards the crashing branches and Aegis turned to see Shank finally catching up, much slower on their humanoid legs than he and Ina. Unwavered by their presence, Mona looked back to Avery with stern command.

"Return to your slumber."

The witches' toes dragged backwards across the dirt, floating backwards the same way they had come and passed a very confused looking Shank. Dumbfounded, they looked down at Ina; she was still staring at the spot the goddess and the Keeper had been standing until they had vanished.

"What happened, Ina?"

"The girls are safe. But the book is gone."

"I can't see a thing."

"Will you wait just a damn minute?"

Yumi struck the match, lighting the candle of the lantern and cast the stone tunnel in a dim light. She looked back at Owen, who looked terribly frightened still. It was hard trying to be sympathetic; after all, he wasn't the one in this pair who was still susceptible to death.

"Why are there escape tunnels anyway?"

Before she answered his question, she began to walk deeper into the tunnel that lay hidden on the eastern section of the royal grounds. It had been quite easy to get to unnoticed: each wing contained a room with an entrance cleverly disguised within something as unsuspecting as a bookcase or wardrobe. She had accessed it through the moving bookcase of the west-wing drawing room.

"There has been tension between Brightloch and Eyon for decades and decades. My ancestors built this in case they decided to strike - we're no match for their hoarded technology. The plan has always been to flee Brightloch and head for the mountains in the northeast, should that ever happen."

"Oh."

They continued in silence, the only sounds were Yumi's footsteps and the occasional drip of water falling from the damp stone above their heads. Once or twice a droplet fell into the opening in her collar behind her neck and a disgusted shiver ran down her spine.

She knew they would be walking for a while, for the castle was in the very heart of Brightloch and her intended exit was an hour walk beyond the wall. By her count, they would pass twenty ladders leading to the surface before they had a safe distance between them and Brightloch.

"If I didn't know better, I would say you cared a lot for Avery," Owen broke the silence with rather invasive commentary. She frowned.

"You're right, you do know better than to pry."

The boy was silent after her biting remark, though it didn't do much to quiet Yumi's mind.

Avery was in danger and she had no time to waste in finding her. Yumi wished the darkness of the tunnel would swallow her, throwing her into another one of Owen's memories of Avery. Anything to see her face, hear her voice. There was nothing for Yumi at the palace when she was out there somewhere.

Frustrated tears pooled in her eyes and she quickly wiped them off with the back of her free hand. Owen caught the moment and peered over at her.

"Do you want to talk about it?"

"No," she said firmly.

He didn't pry any further and she was thankful. They carried on in a long silence, beginning to pass ladders on the sides of the tunnel every once in a while. For nearly an hour they walked before the light of the candle hit a solid wall.

"Did we miss our exit?" Owen didn't seem to understand that their plan had crumbled with the appearance of the solid wall.

Yumi looked upon the wall of stone with a gaping mouth, running forward to examine it closer with the light of the lantern. The tunnel was blocked completely, no hidden door to be found as she frantically ran her hand across the surface.

"I.... I don't understand. We should be able to go so much farther than this. There should be twelve more ladders. I was fucking counting!"

She slapped her hand hard against the wall in frustration, pain throbbing through her whole arm and she grew even more angry with herself for not thinking through her physical reaction a little more carefully.

"Who do you think did this?"

"I don't know, but we're going to have to take the last exit to get out of here."

She turned around, storming back in the direction they had come from with the lantern held just above her head. Her angry heartbeat pounded hard in her ears and she longed to get her hands on whoever had blocked her - and her family's - escape route. Either the Beldam or

Eyon were to blame, she just knew it. When she brought Avery to safety, she would have to make sure to warn her father about the blocked passage.

They came upon the last ladder they had passed and Yumi cradled the thin handle of the lantern in the crook between her index finger and thumb to hold it as she climbed. Though it was heavy, she was able to close her hand around the highest rung she could reach with the lantern still hanging in her grip. She climbed up the ladder hurriedly towards the square of wood at the ceiling of the tunnel.

With one hand holding the lantern and top rung of the ladder, she used her other to unlatch the door and push up carefully. A cold breeze hit her face as she peeked through narrow crack she allowed herself. Through it she saw what appeared to be an empty alleyway, the trotting hooves of a horse clopped from somewhere in front of her followed by the rickety wheels of a carriage.

"No! We're still in Brightloch!"

"Who would have sealed off the tunnel, then?"

Owen's voice came not from beneath her in the tunnel but from above her on the other side of the hidden door. She figured that because he did not warn her, it was safe to come out. Yumi pushed the door open, the false stone hitting the real ones that lined alley ground and she climbed up.

"We're going to just have to cross the wall from the surface," she spoke with a tone she knew was grim as she sealed the hidden door once more. "It won't be easy, but we've been left with no other choices."

Yumi closed her cloak close around her, making sure the hood was secured around her head. Peeking her head out of the alleyway, she saw the street was sparse of any people. Another carriage was heading in the direction opposite of the other, towards where the wall could be seen just above the pine trees that grew denser on the outskirts of town. Once she made it into the trees, she should be safe. From there she could either find a gate or another entry back into the tunnel.

"Keep watch ahead of me. Warn me of anything that looks like it could be a threat," she said before starting in the direction of the eastern wall.

Owen nodded dutifully, running ahead of her. She followed him with a calm pace, doing her best to not attract attention of any kind. It was late in the night, the only people she passed were returning from taverns or too focused on getting home to pay her any mind. Still she kept her eyes forward and her hood drawn close around her face.

The closer to the wall they got, the more the homes and buildings began to drift farther away from each other until the road ended abruptly, giving way to the pine trees without so much as a dividing line. Beyond the treetops stood the wall.

Owen was waiting for her at the hungry mouth of the woods, pausing for any instructions Yumi might have had for him. She looked behind her back towards the town behind them; no one to be seen by and no one to be interrupted by.

"Press on," she said and followed the spirit into the trees.

Once the trees formed a wall behind them, Yumi paused to rekindle her lantern. She held it up to break apart the darkness of the woods as she hurried to catch up to Owen.

She followed the spirit down the hill, the faint glow of the earthen spirits beginning to manifest. The hum of the tree roots beneath her feet grew just loud enough for her to notice, as she watched short and humanoid figures peer down at her from the branches.

"Where are you going, Princess?"

They whispered down with tiny and eerie voices. As unsettling as they had appeared on a first glance, Yumi already knew that they wouldn't harm her. Even the nervous Owen didn't look the slightest bit uncomfortable by their presence; she assumed he could see them, anyway.

"You aren't leaving us, are you Princess?"

"She has to, her witch is in danger!"

This time Yumi did stop, looking up at the tree spirits with the lantern held above her head with an inquisitive stare in her eyes.

"Where did you hear that?"

"From the boy as he passed through here. Our roots reach Sister Od."

Yumi looked at Owen as he stared up at the spirits. He met her look with a shrug. She turned back up to the spirits, watching one small figure swing from one branch to another. Their blue luminescence gave them the appearance of stars as hundreds of spirits looked down on them from the tops of the tallest pines.

"What do you know about Avery- the Berserker Witch?"

"We know of the rage she has sparked in the Beldam, for she has led not one but two of her terrible Knights astray," they answered together with unmoving mouths, Yumi was unable to pinpoint exactly which of them was speaking to her.

"We know of our Father and His desires to shield her. For He heeds not to the slanderous words of man, but to the paths of flawed men who aim to be righteous and true."

"Father, Father!"

They began echoing the word with boisterous love, Yumi and Owen turned around and kept walking to put the noise as far behind them as they could.

"They weren't very helpful, were they?"

Yumi ignored him and kept her focus forward, glancing now and then up at the fewer forest spirits in the trees above them - much quieter than their brethren just west.

"The wall is about two miles ahead of us," she explained. "Once we get there, we can find a gate and cut down any guards in our way. Beyond that and we're home free."

There was a long and weary pause before the dead boy answered her. "I don't like the idea of cutting down men who are just fulfilling their promise to protect. Life is sacred, Yumi. I thought you of all people would understand that."

She stopped, holding the lantern up to see his face clearly. The flicker of the candle wavered in his golden eyes as he looked at her with uncertainty, perhaps with the expectation that she was going to lash out for what he had said. And she felt sorry.

"You're right. By all gods, you're right. No one at that wall deserves to die," she spoke softly and his narrow shoulders eased down in relief. "I'm terribly afraid of what might happen to her."

Owen nodded in sorrowful agreement. "I am, too. But we're going to see her through it, you and me together, even if no one else can."

She smiled to the best of her ability with the given situation. "Thank you, Owen."

He nodded before resuming to his role of ghostly lookout and Yumi followed behind him a few less paces than she had before. They walked the remaining miles with an understood silence that came with the uncertainty of Avery's fate.

Soon the trees ended abruptly where the wall of sarsen sandstone bricks split the woods in half. There was no gate or door of any kind where they had approached it and Yumi held up her lantern, looking from her left to her right.

"Let's just walk this way until we find one of the gates," she instructed, stepping hurriedly to follow the wall southward.

As they scrambled up and down the uneven terrain, the faint mumble of men's voices came into earshot. Yumi froze briefly; they must have been getting close. She strained her eyes looking into the darkness ahead of them, swearing she saw flickers of other lanterns from between the trees.

"How are we going to get past them?"

Owen had whispered as though anyone else around them might hear him and she pursed her lips together in thought.

"As much as you won't like it," she said "I might have to injure them, non-fatally, to get past them. Aside from doing that, look for a gap in the sentinels to slip through. They can't really be anticipating any people leaving at this hour from this route, can they?"

She opened the glass of her lantern, blowing out the half-melted stump of a candle. They stood still for long minutes as Yumi's eyes adjusted to the darkness, only a small amount of the bright moonlight made it through the treetops to allow her to see.

Leaving the lantern behind, they crept up the hill towards where Yumi had seen the lights bouncing back and forth. Finally, they came close enough and from behind a tree she saw an iron gate in the massive stone wall. In front of it were four men, uniformed in navy coats with brass buttons and helmets. Yumi noted that each of them was carrying a sword and she swallowed nervously. Leaving them unscathed would be difficult if they would not want to grant her the same courtesy. Owen looked at her knowingly and she nodded - still, none were to be harmed.

She was then struck by the obvious and she yanked off her hood. Certainly, they would refuse to harm her if they saw that they were dealing with the daughter of King Harthmoor; maybe they would just let her pass through without a fuss.

With newfound confidence in her plan, she crept forward from tree to tree as she approached the gate. She studied the two guards who paced back and forth in a steady circuit, timed their steady footsteps. Thirty seconds from end to end of their rotation, meeting every thirty seconds in the middle. The other two guards stood solid as stone on each side of the gate, looking as serious as a funeral. One of them, if not both, must have the key to the gate with the massive lock in the center.

She sucked in a breath, exhaling in frustration. Of course, it couldn't be easy. Yumi reached into her belt, pulling out her sharpest dagger.

"To wound, not to kill," she reminded herself. *But for Avery...*

She walked straight and proud towards the gate, her dagger in hand but concealed in the folds of her cloak. The two pacing guards stopped and looked at her as though they weren't sure if someone was indeed trying to pass. Their eyes went wide with shocked disbelief when her identity was realized.

"Y-Your Highness, what on earth are you doing out here? And at this hour," one guard stammered in confusion.

"I do not wish to be questioned," she stated, regal and firm. "Please let me pass through this gate without incident."

The guards looked at each other, visibly unsure if they should obey the royal family member who was present or the highest ruling member who had clearly instructed them to never let this one beyond the walls for her own safety.

"Your Highness, I'm afraid we can't let you do that. King Harthmoor had declared in the month of -"

"I know what my father has said," she snapped. Yumi began stepping forward and each guard on the side of the gate took a step forward in disciplined unison.

"Please," she said softer "just let me through. I don't want to hurt any of you."

Three out of the four guards looked confused; the man on the right edge of the gate looked as though he might be stifling back a laugh. Yumi frowned. Whatever happened was out of her hands now.

Gut them, little Knight.

The Knight inside her growled the gruesome encouragement and Yumi lunged forward, her dagger in her hand held across her body protectively as she ran towards the gate. The two roving guards reached for her with their free hands, and Yumi slashed and them wildly as she pushed through.

She screamed in frustration as one guard closed a hand around her arm, trying to push her down to the ground. Yumi spun in his grip trying to break free and slashed her dagger across his shoulder. He reeled backwards in surprise, looking at his comrade in confusion as to what they should do. Injure the Princess?

As the other two guards closed in on her, she used her elbows to try to shove her way out of the circle formed around her. Which one of them had the key? She looked frantically at each of them, not a key around their neck nor on their person to be seen. Yumi slashed again, trying to push them back.

A hand shot out and grabbed her by the wrist, twisting it around and the strain on her muscles caused the dagger to fall from her fingers. With her free hand she swung, trying her best to land a punch anywhere on any of the men. She punched at empty air until one guard gently pushed at the back of her knee with his, sending her tumbling to the ground.

"Go sound the bell for backup. We need to get her back to the castle and explain what has happened here," one guard said and the roving guard she had struck first vanished into the night.

In the space he left, Yumi looked up from the ground at where Owen had watched the whole thing. His face was painted in grief as he looked down upon her, unable to do anything to help. Yumi began to weep.

She had failed.

CHAPTER NINE

TWO OF SWORDS

Balthazar waited in the thick fog with his wife. The only sign of the sunrise underneath was the eerie glow that crept over the cliffs of Eyon, somewhere beyond the Stillmaw Sea. Mona's stare was grave as she watched the temple of crumbling marble for signs of movement with her grimoire clutched above her pregnant belly.

"They said they would be here," she whispered, not turning to look at him. "Has my own family betrayed me?"

He chose his words carefully before speaking, placing his hand gently on her warm umber shoulder.

"Believe me, Queen, if they wished to go to the efforts of turning on one of their own it wouldn't be you."

If the Oracles of Neri chose to lure anyone into a trap, it would be him; not the beloved Goddess of Witches. They were skeptical of his stance on the Knights of Od and it had been their demand that Mona arrive with the grimoire in-hand, stolen back and out of reach of a Knight. What had they seen in their visions?

The temple porch stirred with movement as figures emerged. Balthazar dropped his hand and Mona straightened up, eager to keep her poised and unafraid appearance. The hooded oracles crossed the garden of overgrown thicket that once bloomed with asters and snapdragons this late in the summer. Their ruby red cloaks floated past long-dry fountains; the humans had let a sanctuary that even Balthazar found beautiful go to a sorrowful waste.

In a row of five, the oracles stopped before Balthazar and Mona. They bowed and Balthazar knew that the gesture was not for him, but his goddess wife. When they stood upright again, the figure in the middle lowered their hood.

The man was young, perhaps only a few decades old at most. A stripe of sky-blue was painted from the bottom lobe of his ear, across his nose, and to the other ear; the ritual painting was striking against his tawny flesh.

"I hope to hear that you have brought the grimoire."

The oracle spoke with a gentle command even as he looked upon the book clutched to Mona's chest, wanting her to confirm it with certainty.

"The genuine grimoire. The decoy, I imagine, is still somewhere in Od," Mona answered, her words unusually quick and nervous.

The oracle smiled. "That is wonderful news! I am sure you understand what a large step this is in our goal to end the Knights. It was too much of a risk to keep it within reach of the Knight of Water. He poses as an ally, but demons cannot be trusted so easily."

Balthazar grimaced; the oracle did not apologize.

"It will not be enough to simply enact the spell in the grimoire," the man shifted on his feet, his mood becoming stern as he spoke with a furrowed brow. "We must kill the vessels of all Knights to ensure that resurrection is not an option for the Beldam or Paion. I feel that-"

"Listen here, squirt," Balthazar cut him off, unable to listen to any more of the absurdity. "No one's resurrecting the Knights, they will be dust. I find it a little insulting that you insinuate the Goddess of Witches would leave a loose end."

The oracle glared at him, his dark irises flickering with interest as though Balthazar had offered him a challenge.

"We have to ensure the end of the Knights by cutting off all routes. If they don't kill each other in the aftermath, you must do it. If we can rid the Knights of these vessels, well, I'll make sure Neri puts in a good word to Ara about your *offspring*. Any vision she has about the child can mean life or death."

As the oracle spoke with an icy cold voice, he eyed Mona's belly and Balthazar inhaled with seething rage but held in the words he wished to say; they've been played. Even Mona was speechless, her lips parted as she stared at the oracle in horror. Ara, the Goddess of All, could so easily prevent their child from being born a demon and it weighed on whether the vessels for the Knights died.

"I am certain that you will make the clearly righteous decision," the oracle said as he lifted the crimson hood back over his head, his face as darkly concealed as his colleagues' were.

Without another word, they turned and retreated through the garden and disappeared through the temple's front doors. Balthazar and Mona stood in such a heavy silence that the faint sound of the waves crashing against the cliffs reached Balthazar's ears.

Mona turned and looked at him, her eyes sorrowful.

"We don't have a choice."

Balthazar looked down at the bump of Mona's womb, then down at the ground. This was not at all how he wanted to be welcomed into the good graces of the gods. It was the vessels or his child.

"I'm sorry, William," he murmured.

Avery's eyes fluttered open when the early sunbeams of morning reached her face. She held her hand over her sleepy eyes while they were temporarily blinded.

When Avery adjusted her vision and lowered her hand, she caught sight of a flickering movement in the trees.

She froze up in fright, slowly moving her hand to reach for where Hemlock had laid beside her as she slept. Avery looked around at the other Reapers; she was the first one in their group who was awake and alert. When she looked up, a blur of brown flickered again and she caught sight of the buck's head in the brush as it carefully stepped uphill.

Avery sank back against the tree again when she realized it was only an animal and she sucked in a relieved breath. She sat still for a moment, watching the buck dip its head low to the ground and then back again. As Avery watched from across the distance, she noticed gashes of red around the top and sides of the buck's head.

Avery debated for a moment whether she should get closer to the animal and assess the injuries, leaning forward to get up when she decided it was the right thing to do.

"Where are you going?"

Avery stopped and looked in Shank's direction. They were sitting upright under their blanket and looked from Avery to the buck.

"It's injured," she whispered. "I was going to see if I could leave it some water and-"

Shank cut her off with a laugh. "Avery, he's fine. He's just shedding his velvet."

She paused. "His what?"

"Bucks have layers of velvet around their antlers. Around late summer when their antlers harden, the velvet is shed in a rather bloody mess. It happens every year and doesn't hurt them."

Avery didn't answer them, feeling embarrassed that she didn't know. She sank lower against the tree, her canvas backpack tugging against the bark. Something felt different. Her eyes widened and she shot up to her feet as she threw her backpack off.

"Where is it?"

Avery paid no mind to the volume of her shout as she rummaged through the rucksack for the missing grimoire. She dumped the contents onto the ground as the Reapers around her stirred, awoken by her commotion.

"Where's what?"

Maria rubbed her eyes as she asked, as groggy and confused as everyone else.

"Mona's spell book is gone!"

"*Balthazar.*"

Avery dropped her bag and looked to where Aegis was stretching, leaning far on his back haunches with his front legs reaching in front of him. The black cat sat upright as though to dignify himself after being caught yawning and he looked at Avery as though she was supposed to know what he had meant.

"What do you mean 'Balthazar'? What did he do?"

"*He and Mona crept in last night when you were all sleeping and took it back. Be it a spell or hypnosis, he lured you to them and took it back. I daresay he is still a little miffed about yesterday.*"

Avery rubbed her hand down her face, tugging her eyelids down in frustration before dropping her arm.

"Fucking… Balthazar. How are we supposed to get it back? How are we supposed to stop the Knights like *they* want if they stole the spell?"

"*It sounds like you'll get it back when you're in Eyon. Maybe before that. They wanted to remove the leverage you all have over them. I can't be terribly mad; I likely would have done the same thing.*"

"You would have done that because you're an asshole."

"*Guilty as charged.*"

Avery huffed and turned her frustration away from the familiar, bending down to stuff her dumped possessions back into her rucksack.

"Sorry Ave," Shank said as they stood up and folded their blanket. "I was actually just about to tell you. Ina and I tried to stop him, but with Mona there…"

She stopped and looked up at Shank as he offered an apologetic smile.

"Don't worry about it," she mumbled, a little grumpier than she had intended to sound. "We know where to find Moz. We'll get it when we need it, I assume. Not much we can do about it anyway until the bastard dares to show his face again."

After Avery told the rest of the group what had happened, they finished packing up their belongings and left the campsite. The sun glided across the sky from behind them as they headed west. From time to time they would stop, waiting for Grim to catch up as he followed on his stout, reptilian legs. *Gods, how does Cassie get anywhere with that hulking beast?*

"What's that up there?"

Avery's gaze followed the direction Cassie pointed in, her pace quickening to identify the still shapes of grey standing in their path.

The columns of sarsen sandstone towered over the ferns and grasses, holding up nothing but the dust-speckled sunbeams that were able to find their way to the forest floor through the thick canopies overhead. Crumbling steps led up to a circular platform where a young ash tree attempted to grow within the giant cracks of the stone slab.

Theirrin's grizzly stood upright, casting a shadow over Avery and Lily while he sniffed at the air with his front paws held at his sides. Avery's attention was caught briefly by a monarch butterfly fluttering across her periphery before she looked back at the other Reapers, ready to ask them if they were familiar with their whereabouts.

The ground beneath them creaked and groaned as the roots of the trees encompassing them began to stir. Dirt bulged beneath Avery's boots and she hurried backwards to get away, stumbling into Lily until her sister followed in frightened retreat.

A blanket of earth was pulled back as tree roots whipped into the air, entangling themselves to form an entirely new trunk. The trunk began to take on a humanoid shape, long roots turning to finger-like twigs easily the length of Avery's entire arm.

The earth birthed a giant made of the trees, cloaked in the mosses and the ferns of the forest floor cascaded down its back. A buck skull with its ten-point antlers that had been buried intact somewhere deep beneath their feet was perched atop the shoulders of root mass, white eyes glowing within the orbital cavities.

"Malo, Lord of the Forest," Tristan said breathlessly from somewhere behind her.

The glowing eyes looked down at Avery as the god lifted five spindly branches to lay his hand upon her. She stood still, not wanting to make any unpredicted movements to avoid being crushed by the tree limbs.

Avery found herself entranced in his stare as the lord closed his entire hand around her head; the shouts of her friends and even the cries of the grizzly behind her were muffled to complete silence as the tree roots embraced her.

Her breathing began to grow shallow and quick, panic rising as she stood in complete darkness and silence. She waited for Malo's grip to crush her, wondering why she remained unharmed. What was his intention if not to kill her?

When the idea of immediate death no longer seemed to be a threat, Avery realized that lying just under the silence of isolation was the sound of the roots creaking and whispering amongst themselves. Their language was one she couldn't understand and though their voices were eerily like the voices of the demon fledgling orbs, a sense of calmness settled in her shoulders. Malo's body - though frightening - teemed with the life of the wood.

The coffin of earth around her held comforting warmth and she found her breathing slowing to its calm pace. A faint green light emerged from the dense tangle of plant matter. A firefly bobbed into the cavity around Avery's head, casting the chamber in a bright green glow as three more followed it. She lifted her hand up to hold one of the lightning bugs on her fingers and instead of bobbing back into the darkness, the insect fluttered closer to her face and her field of vision became aglow.

Tears welled up in Avery's eyes and spilled over, rolling across her grin. The tangible interaction with the god overwhelmed her with a feeling of love and a bizarre peace with the idea that death had been so close; in death this was where she would return.

The chamber swirled with warm air from the outside as Malo's grip released her, the Lord straightening back up to His full height as He looked down on her. Avery understood then that what she had received was a blessing of some kind - there was no other way to explain the calm feeling that had suddenly overcome her.

Malo dipped His head, the stag skull bobbing once in a bow and Avery bowed deep with new devotion. When she stood upright, Malo reached with outstretched branches towards Tristan. His eyes flickered nervously from the forest Lord to Avery, allowing the branches to encircle him only after he was reminded that Avery was released without harm. The tree-hands encircled the large man as though he were just as small as Avery.

After a long moment, the exorcist was released. His breathing was deep and labored, but sheer happiness was spread across his face when he looked upon Malo.

The man and the god exchanged low bows before Malo moved on.

Alice dodged the wiry hand when it reached for her, panic alight in her golden eyes as she lifted her handgun. Brandishing a gun towards a literal god? Avery wondered what made Alice so afraid despite two people being not only unharmed, but joyous.

Vinny shrank back to stand behind Alice, not wanting Malo to touch him either. She didn't understand how they could feel panic when the presence of the Lord of the Forest held her in a strangely warm comfort. Though there was no way to read the Lord's expression, the air of confusion was obvious as His hand retreated and He straightened upright once again.

Cassie looked at her friend in bewilderment, grabbing Rowan by the hand and pulling him forward with her. The boy looked frightened as ever and Cassie held her grip steady as Malo leaned forward again and laid His hand upon their heads, encompassing them entirely with root before releasing them. Even Rowan looked elated, tears running down his toothy grin and off his chin.

Even after Malo had blessed everyone present, Alice remained firm with her handgun between the god and the child. Kurosaki gently nudged her shoulder as though to make sure she didn't have any second thoughts, but she said nothing to recant her refusal.

Malo stepped backwards onto the stone platform, watching only Alice with tense silence as His roots slapped up against the stone, devouring the steps in his wake. The roots began to wrap around the infant ash tree and Malo stretched upwards even higher as His limbs shot out into more narrow branches.

The Reapers watched in silence as the god compressed Himself into a taller ash tree, taking over where the smaller had stood unimpressively. A stag skull fell from the sky, shattering on the tangle of roots and stone. Bone dust was carried on the next breath of the breeze; Malo had vanished as suddenly has He had appeared.

Avery found that she was still standing frozen in awe, she looked upon the sarsen altar and then back to the rest of the Reapers. Tristan appeared to be the most ecstatic, joyous tears on his face as he spun in a circle to look for any other gods that may decide to grace them with their presence.

"Tristan," Maria called to his attention gently with the sleeve of his shirt pinched between her fingers. "We need to go. Moz needs us."

He looked from the treetops down to his much-shorter friend. His face suddenly turned from glee to sincere sadness and he wrapped his arms around Maria's head in what was perhaps supposed to have been a hug. Maria pounded her fist on Tristan's chest, trying to wriggle free, but the stronger man wanted to hug more than she desired to break free and she allowed herself to be held.

"Y'know how much this would have meant to Moz if he was here."

A pang of sadness hit Avery and she looked down at the red cord around her neck. The clapperless bell was the hard proof of just how much Malo's blessing would have meant to Moz. If there was a way she could make it happen for him too, she would.

A set of fingers slid into hers and Avery looked up at Lily. She nodded with knowing eyes and Avery knew that Lily didn't need to hear her words to understand that she was worried. Lily then turned to the rest of the group.

"Well the sooner we get him, the better, right? Let's keep going. It feels like we're almost there!"

Tristan let go of the suffocating hug around Maria's skull, she stumbled backwards and gasped for air. He jumped off his heels to jolt his rucksack up higher on his back and fumbled to feel where his sword was secured to the strap as though he may have somehow lost it.

"I reckon you're right, Lily. The time's about right and we're up steeper hills - we must be near Brightloch."

The group marched west and found that Tristan's observations were correct - Avery felt her climbing becoming more vertical with every passing hour until she had to use her hands to help her scramble up rocks. She found herself again envious of Aegis hitching a ride in her rucksack and seriously contemplated putting him on the ground with them out of petty spite.

"Walking is for mortals and dogs."

Avery scowled. When they reached the peak of the small mountain, she ripped the canteen out of her bag and stopped for a drink. Beside her, Lily stopped with both of her hands on her hips and peered past the pines at the sea of green below them.

"Now I see…. why Brightloch is so damn rich," she heaved between breaths. "Mining and logging."

Avery handed Lily her canteen, who took it eagerly and sloshed water down her chin as she drank. Usually manner-conscious, she didn't seem to care about the soaked spot on her tunic as she handed back the vessel.

"Look, over there," Theirrin interrupted, pointing forward at a plume of smoke coming from somewhere beyond the next mountain.

"We're close."

Instead of the excitement Avery had expected from Maria to be so close to rescuing Moz, her expression looked grim as she looked upon the smoke. Silence fell upon the group, thick with fear as to what awaited them just over the ridge.

CHAPTER TEN

THE HANGED MAN

T hat must be the prison," Tristan murmured with a finger pointed towards the grey compound tucked against the foot of the mountain. "I reckon it's underground as well."

Avery turned around and looked at Theirrin for confirmation. The younger girl nodded her head, her face pulled into a firm and cold frown with obvious distaste for where they were.

She looked forward again and quickly scanned the exterior. The façade was a single story and unimpressive, matching grey watchtowers flanking each side of it. Lily stuck her head over Avery's shoulder from where she crouched in the bushes.

"So, what's our plan, bone brigade?"

"We go in, kill 'em all. You can snap open the lock tumblers," Avery answered as though it was the most rational solution in the world.

Lily frowned. "That is incredibly and stupidly simple."

"I must admit it's been working so far," Maria interjected with a shrug.

Behind her, Avery heard the mechanical snapping and clicks of Alice and Kurosaki loading their guns. They only used their limited supply of bullets when they deemed it absolutely necessary; rescuing Moz was as important to them as it was to her. Only days before, they were considering unloading their clips on Moz when they found out he was the Knight and Avery couldn't help but wonder what it was exactly that had changed their minds.

Avery looked to Theirrin. "Thanks for all of your help, it really means a lot to us."

Theirrin nodded, already scuttling backwards across the rocks to lead her group back in the direction they had come from. "We'll keep our ears open should you need us again. Good luck."

Avery watched them leave until the end of Grim's tail disappeared into the thick brush and turned to look at the group behind her.

"Is everyone ready?"

"As ready as I can be," Lily grumbled, her stare fixed on the prison with unease.

"Don't worry, I always got your back."

Lily looked at her with a half-smile, not looking at all convinced. Quickly, Maria leaned forward and pecked Lily on the cheek.

"Me too."

Kurosaki snorted with laughter from behind them. "Don't act like it'll be the last fight, or it will be. No need-"

He was cut off with a yelp when Alice elbowed him in the ribs. Kurosaki's startle turned playful and he flicked one of the buns of hair on Alice's head; clearly, he wasn't worried at all about storming the prison. Avery tried to take solace in his demeanor, but as she watched the subtle flickers of movement outside the fortress, she couldn't say she felt as easy as he did. Shoving the feeling away, for Moz's sake, she turned back to face the group.

"Here's the plan."

The battle tactic was laid out thoroughly. Holes left by Avery's relative inexperience were filled by Alice and Kurosaki - ironically by filling everything in sight with bullet holes.

"Leave only Mozzy alive," Alice said, encouraging Lily and Avery to rise.

Lily stood up first, rising slowly from the brush with her bow held in her relaxed hand. Avery rose with her and carefully emerged from the brush, twirling her grip around Hemlock's end as she readied herself for the cut. The sound of firearms loading and sliding formed a safety net behind her and Avery tried to let herself relax. Barrels from the snipers' guns jutted out from their hiding place in the brush as Alice and Kurosaki lay flat against the ground.

When the snipers were locked and loaded, the silence among the Reapers was filled by gentle wind rolling through the firs and pines. The brushing needles were the sweetest melody to Avery's ears and she sucked in a breath to take in as much of it as she could. She thought of the forest god and His massive buck skull, taking her into His giant hand with sinking relief.

"Help us, Malo," Avery said softly.

With a sharp slash, her palm was ripped open by the blade meant for Paion. Her eyes glazed over white and the world around her grew a little dimmer as the world of the dead leaked into hers. The spirits rose from the ground in front of the two witches, ready to kill.

Avery stepped forward, her right hand gripped tight by Lily's. Her left hand dripped blood, spilling down onto Hemlock's hilt.

"Avery, I'm a loose cannon with this thing. Do you trust me?"

Lily's voice shook when she asked, but Avery's did not when she answered.

"With my life. Always."

Avery squeezed Lily's hand once more before transferring her sword to her dominant hand. They walked into the open expanse that lay between them and the prison. Shouts rose from the parapet walls as the Legion officers spotted the two witches.

In groups of five, the uniformed henchmen worked together to steer iron cannons in Avery and Lily's direction. Avery resisted the urge to look behind her; she had to trust that the rest of her friends were not in the line of fire without giving them away.

Lily held her hands up and with a strained sweep of her arms, the cannons turned off the witches to blast holes in the fortress key behind the parapet wall.

The wide grated door screeched open and Legion officers came spilling out in a flock of grey. Avery looked over her shoulder and past Lily. They were the only obstacle in the way.

"Hit the ground!" Avery hollered, loud enough for both Lily and the snipers to hear.

The two women threw themselves flat onto the dirt just before the rapid fire of bullets ripped through the officers. Their bodies jerked and spattered before hitting the ground in front of Avery. Beyond their corpses lay the open door that would lead them to Moz.

An officer in the pile of limbs groaned, hanging onto life by a fragile thread. Avery crawled forward, shimmying her elbows and knees to keep as low to the earth as possible. A man with ginger hair and galaxies of freckles across his nose coughed up blood, but his eyes still blinked as he laid on his back. He was very much alive still.

Avery stopped and began to extend her swinging arm, wondering if she could gather enough force to finish the job without getting shot herself.

"Avery," Lily hissed from behind her. Avery paused, but did not turn. Her grip on Hemlock tightened.

"He's neutralized, he won't be standing between us getting Moz," her sister continued. "To kill him now is for the sake of murder."

The gunfire stopped and Avery heard Kurosaki's shouts from behind them.

"Go, go, go!"

The long-range Reapers fled their hiding place to join Lily and Avery once the path inside the prison had been cleared for them.

"I reckon you might be the love o' Moz's life after he hears about this," Tristan teased as he passed Avery.

Avery's cheeks flushed red as she scrambled up out of the dirt. She was determined to be the one leading Moz's rescue and she pushed through the pack of Reapers to dive into the prison sword-first. Avery was the reason he was somewhere within the stone walls and it was her responsibility to make sure he made it out unharmed.

They stormed the stone hallway that was cast in a burning glow from the lanterns. Avery's rage flared from flickers to flames as the first rush of Legion officers charged their entrance.

A man who also wielded a broadsword lurched in her direction and Avery deflected with a crash of metal, pushing him towards the wall. Her shadowy revenants leaped upon him, closing their dark fingers around his throat and jerking his head until bone crunched. His body thumped into a heap and remained still on the floor as the officers behind him began to fill with bullets and arrows.

Avery's ego inflated, rising to meet her rage and she grinned. "Better call for back-up, it's the goddamn Berserker Witch."

The light stretched across the cell floor, searing his pupils before he could squeeze his eyes shut. An outline of a body burned on the back of his eyelids, an image of the woman who waited in the open door. He tried to shrink away from her but was useless in the chains that held him against the damp wall.

They would creep into his damp cell like thieves in the night, circling around the knowledge he had been able to keep hidden for so long. *Where is the last Knight? Where do we find them?*

They had used glamour spells, wearing Avery's face, to trick him into speaking in between attempts to beat the information out of him. He never once let his guard down; he relived a rescue night after night until Morgana slammed the cell shut again and left him in darkness.

The boots stepped forward and he waited with his eyelids still blocking everything out. He would never again give them the satisfaction of giving him hope before yanking it away again.

"Moz?"

Moz. Not William, *Moz*. The name his friends called him, he saw their faces so clearly, as bright as the sun in his own skull. Fingers cool as death touched his cheek and he opened his eyes. The palm connected to it was endlessly slashed, some of the cuts aged and scarred pink. He couldn't see her face, but this time he knew. It was *her*.

Her hand pulled away and he struggled to turn his neck to see what was happening. She pulled a metal canteen out from her bag and held a handful of fabric from the corner of her cloak against the open container to soak it.

"A... Avery," he choked.

"Don't worry, I've got you. Just drink," Avery said, using her right hand to hold the canteen to his mouth and the left to mop the dried blood off his face. "Lily, get the locks."

Moz had not even seen the people behind Avery. The locked cuffs around his wrists snapped open and clattered to the ground. He toppled over, his muscles unable to hold him upright without the chain forcing him. Avery hastily capped the canteen and tossed it aside, leaning forward with an arm looped under his shoulder to try to help him back upright.

"Tristan, help!"

The light from the outside hall was blocked when Tristan's giant frame stepped in front of Moz, wrapping an arm under his shoulders and the other at the base of his spine. Nausea washed over Moz as the world spun around and he was suddenly upright again. His knees buckled under him after days of sitting in one position. Moz almost collapsed again until another arm swooped under him to hold him upright.

The canteen again was forced to his lips and this time he was finally able to get water from the nearly empty bottle. He was given no water at all in the cell and he drank gratefully until it was empty.

"Come on, we have to go," Avery said as she put the canteen away, turning to leave the cell.

She had already disappeared around the corner before Tristan and Shank began dragging him from beneath his aching shoulders. He opened his mouth to call out, but it was still only a raspy whisper.

"I... need her."

"Don't worry, she knows!"

Shank's comment would have warranted a scowl at the least, but Moz was beyond exhaustion. They carried him out into the dim hall of the prison and he braced himself for another impact to the face, but none came; Avery had swept the place clean.

Her back was to him as she spoke next to Lily in a hushed tone. Moz struggled to call out her name once more. Avery turned, her expression firm with determination but a small flash of a smile seemed to be just for him.

"You can thank me after we're safe and far from here," she beamed.

Alice and Kurosaki followed behind Avery and Lily, the gun in Alice's hands sweeping side to side with each corridor they passed. Kurosaki moved as a unit with her, familiar and completely in sync with the lilac-haired force of mayhem.

Dull shouts came from somewhere above them, no doubt from the Legion soldiers on the floor above them as news of the prison break spread. Moz's friends in front of him looked upwards in reaction to the sound, pressing forward with their weapons held high. Avery looked over her shoulder at him with another flash of a sincere smile and he knew that he was going to be okay.

When Avery turned, she cut her hand with Hemlock and her hair floated upwards in his unsteady vision. Uniformed bodies darted out from corridors and the blurry revenants slashed at their skin, Avery charging in after them with a loud cry as she threw all her might behind her sword. She slashed the nearest man mercilessly into the gut, not stopping to watch him sputter blood as he sank to his knees.

Avery Porter was not a woman, she was a force to be reckoned with. Her hurricanes gave no sailor time to batten down the hatches and wreaked havoc of all who chose to stand in her way. Gods, he loved her so.

Shank and Tristan continued to carry his weight, and Moz's feet dragged past the face-down body she had cut down.

Beside Avery, Lily marched with her bow and fired arrows; she gracefully swept an arm low to rip them out of wounded men as she passed. Bodies flew out of their path, Lily's focused stare locked around Legion necks and twisted with a sickening snap. He remembered the sudden unlatching of the locks at her request - she must have dealt with Balthazar, too.

Let me take the wheel, Mozzy-boy. I'll make you strong, too.

"Get me … in a space big enough, and I'll do it," he croaked, acknowledging the Knight out loud for the first time. Shank looked down at him with puzzlement, no doubt confused by the answer to a question they didn't hear.

A faint roll of thunder came from somewhere above their heads, beyond the cramped stone ceiling, and the demon inside him laughed throatily.

I knew you would begin to see things my way.

Ahead of him, Kurosaki fired three shots into a Legion officer and Moz felt bizarrely flattered that Kurosaki would use his rationed ammo for his jailbreak. He watched a giddy grin spread across his pale face and his deep-set brown eyes were wide with excitement.

Look at your friends having all the fun while we get dragged along. Let me be your limbs.

He didn't question the voice that time, shrugging out of the grips on his arms. Moz stumbled on his weak legs as he tried to walk on his own.

"Are you sure you can walk?" Shank asked.

Moz didn't answer, striding forward to stop the rest of the group before they entered a stairwell.

"Kurosaki… I'd like my sword back."

Kurosaki turned his toothy grin in his direction, lowering his gun long enough to take Moz's sheathed sword off his back to toss it to him. Moz drew the white sword before putting the sheath back on and the familiar weight of it instantly made him feel whole again.

All that was missing was the tiny demon - where was Jack? Moz didn't think he could communicate with him with the Knight taking the front seat, there seemed to only be room for one of them at a time. He trusted that his friends had kept his small familiar safe and this wasn't the time to go digging for the rat.

Avery disappeared up and into the stairwell with Lily. Moz pushed past Alice and Kurosaki to follow them close behind. Since when did he become so desperate to keep her in his sights during battle? He didn't care but felt more at ease when the sight of her rucksack and sheath came back into view when he reached the top step.

A strange rush propelled his limbs, as though someone else was willing him to move faster - the Knight. They came to an empty corridor leading outside through a broken grate doorway as a uniformed body scurried out into the sunlight. *Where is everyone?*

Outside, preparing for you. For us.

It made sense - they would be eager to battle the Knight. He had to admit he was eager to get Morgana in her vulnerable form, the only opportunity to kill her was when she let the Knight take over. Moz certainly became vulnerable as well; but that was a chance he was willing to take after fighting for so long.

He watched Avery step outside and bound down the short steps in a single leap with her cloak of emerald flapping behind her. Moz looked beyond her and smiled; disappointed that he would not get his chance with Morgana but was satisfied with what he found instead.

Peter watched him from the middle of the field, standing out from the fleet with his reflective spectacles.

"How long were you gonna keep me in there, Pete?" He hollered angrily as he brushed past Avery to stand at the head of their group. Moz received no answer from across the empty space.

Moz heard the stirring of the other Knight, a rush of air whipped his coat when the terrible thing living inside Peter awoke just as Lily spread to the right flank of their inverted V-formation.

"*My witch.*"

The opposing demon spoke, calling out to all other Knights who may have been listening when Lily pulled back her arrow. Peter made no move at her threat of arrow fire and Moz knew he had heard correctly; the Knight of Air had chosen Lily as his witch, just as his had chosen Avery. In all honesty, Lily had just become the safest person in the storm brewing on that field. Watching another Knight become wrapped around a witch's finger cleared the fog of confusion he felt when his own Knight called to Avery and Moz could have laughed at the far-fetched idea that latching on - like Balthazar did to Mona - would save them.

"Where's Morgana," Moz spoke, giving away no indication that he had overheard Peter's Knight. "I was hoping we could finally put an end to this bullshit."

"I was wishing for the same thing," Peter called back and Moz scowled. He lifted his sword, pointing it in Peter's direction.

"I imagine killing you will hold me over until she gets back."

"Think about this William. Look at your party, and then look at mine. Are your friends' lives really worth losing? How about the lives of the children we found outside the complex?"

Children? What was he talking about?

He saw the muzzled and chained grizzly bear before he saw the children bound by rope led out from the trees - Peter had held them under control as though he knew Moz would escape. Moz's blood chilled in every vein. A set-up. All of it.

A tall, blonde girl stood at the head of the cuffed group, watching him with angry eyes - she knew he was responsible. Another head poked out from behind her, his eyes went wide with recognition.

The alligator girl is a little far from home, isn't she?

It was so long ago that she and her reptile familiar tried to prevent Moz from entering the swamps of Wrencrest; her eyes were blindfolded with a black cloth, but he'd recognize that flower-dye pastel mop of hair anywhere. She was thrashing her head forward and back as though to use the momentum to knock off the blindfold that only she wore.

Avery was suddenly beside him with Hemlock held high and pointed towards Peter.

"YOU LET THEM GO NOW!" She ordered in a fierce scream.

"If William comes willingly, they will be pardoned. All of your friends will be pardoned."

For a moment, Moz believed him. For as long as it took him to know that Avery was included in that pardon,

Moz saw this as the undeniable truth and the option he should undoubtedly take. He then remembered who he was dealing with - a brother in an oath he didn't volunteer to take, whose word could not be trusted in the slightest.

"Not today and not tomorrow, either," Moz said and spat.

"I care not then if your friends have been Saved. And to them, I beseech you. Do you not see how William has led you to your deaths? He lured each of you from your homes to fight his battle. Do you not see how you are not the first Reapers whose deaths he will be responsible for? If I-"

"SHUT UP," Moz growled, his sword held in front of him with a tighter, angrier grip.

But the Knight of Air did not stop his verbal assault. "Do you think I enjoy cutting down the Reapers you throw at us, Mosley? All of these people could benefit from the lack of distinct life and death and they end up dead because you were too selfish. Because you were too bull-headed to admit that you were wrong. They all had departed loved ones who I am absolutely certain they would have given anything to see again while still in the realm of the living. Do you even remember Anansie?

Merridan? Or do you forget their names after you've used them up? Will you only care after you have gotten your beloved mage killed?"

Moz couldn't bring himself to look at the faces of his friends and instead found himself screaming with unhindered rage. A dull blow to the head knocked him forward and the Knight quickly overcame him. He didn't feel the pain of his body being folded inside the snapping sinews and bones growing from him, didn't feel the Knight unfurl its enormous wings. Moz shrunk backwards, taking the backseat of his own brain as though watching through someone else's eyes.

He watched as the Knight snatched up a Legion officer between its jaws, heard the crunch of bones between grinding teeth and the thud of the mangled corpse drop to the ground. The Reapers behind Peter stepped backwards without him, unsure of what to do as they waited for their leader to transform as well. Peter looked up at him with a grin of glee, eager to strike at Moz now that he was vulnerable.

"And believe me," Peter added as he calmly took off his glasses, folded them neatly, and put them in the breast pocket of his coat, "she will die."

We need the witch. Need the witch. Witch.

The small part of Moz that still glowed inside of the body of the beast prayed that Avery understood she couldn't jump head first into this one; prayed that she would hang back and protect her friends. Whatever she did in that field, she needed to ignore the call of the demon.

The Knight didn't have to wait long for Peter to engage. His Reaper form exploded and expanded until his place was taken by a skeletal beast much like his, inky black in the places where Moz was sapphire. Peter did not wait a single moment before crashing headfirst into Moz, the horns atop their heads clashing and tangling as they tried to be the first to overpower the other.

He snapped at Peter, trying to close his large jaws around the Knight's throat. His attack was evaded and the Knight of Air launched upwards into the sky. Moz quickly followed into the low-hanging clouds and thunder rumbled from all directions as they began to unleash a downpour of rain and roaring wind.

— ❧ —

Avery cut her palm on the edge of Hemlock. The witch Balthazar had sculpted her into awakened with the stirring of the spirits.

"Lily, can you free them?" Avery yelled over the howling wind and pointed towards the younger Reapers, bound together in a line by rope.

Lily shook her head. "Not from here! If I can't see it, I can't move it! Get me closer!"

Avery wanted to hesitate, to tell her friend to stay somewhere safe. Instead she nodded.

"Follow me!"

Avery began carving a path towards the Reaper children, violently cutting down those Legion members that her angry revenants had missed. Arrows soared from close behind her as Lily followed. Onja of Victory had truly blessed them with Lily's magic; Avery was certain her arrows wouldn't find their way through the gales without a little extra guidance.

"I think I'm close enough!" Lily called out and the sound of her footsteps behind Avery had stopped. "Keep going, we need to get them!"

Avery didn't waste time to voice her agreement as she put distance and bodies between her and her best friend. The rope binding the children began to quake but was still binding them tightly.

"You can do it Lily!" Avery shouted, knowing the pressure and exhaustion her friend was feeling. Avery saw a flash of lilac in her periphery, darting towards the Legion front line as the snapping of gunshots split the air.

She followed Alice as she ran towards a Legion member who wielded a large axe as he strode towards the captive children with his foul gaze fixed on Vinny. The boy broke his stern air to cry out for help, but Avery and Alice were too late. The man wrought his axe down, cutting through the boy's skull as though it were mere paper.

His friends cried out in unhinged horror as they were yanked down towards the ground by the rope still tied around the dead weight. Cassie was beside Vinny and fell over completely, struggling to pull herself out of the mud and spatter without the use of her arms. Avery froze, shocked by the scene as Alice continued to run ahead.

Alice fired again, missing her mark and grunting loud with frustration. With her intense focus on saving the rest of the children, Alice had missed the Legion swordsman who closed in on her faster than any of the

Reapers could have predicted. Avery screamed out a warning, but it did not stop the body from barreling into Alice.

"ALICE!"

The sword plunged through Alice's middle and resurfaced from her back. She froze in shock, looking upon her attacker with pleading eyes as blood began to dribble over her bottom lip and down her small chin. The handgun she held slipped from her fingers, the whimsical bell charm jingling as Alice fell into silence forever. The swordsman yanked the weapon hard out of her, gore and blood splattering before she tumbled to the earth and became lifeless.

"ALICE!"

Avery cried out again, but she knew no response would come.

Kurosaki cried out in agony, emptying his clip at every Legion body as he tried to run to Alice's body. He swung his aim to the man who had killed Alice, screaming out with pained fury as three rounds turned the swordsman's skull to a pulp.

He fired four more in searing rage. His next bullet found the executioner looming over Vinny's body and

Cassie, firing another two until his heavy mass hit the ground. Kurosaki lowered his gun, looking with wide and wild eyes.

Avery was able to clear a path first as the revenants strangled those she did not cut down; she hoped Kurosaki would see the opening and follow. Kurosaki shot at the remaining Legion members seeking to finish the work of the executioner before following her, gunning down anyone who dared approach his fallen friend and her weapons.

From across the fray Avery saw Cassie wriggle in her ropes, dragging her face across the gory ground to free herself of the blindfold. With success, the cloth and her goggles fell to her collarbone and she lifted her face out of the spattered mess. The tears streaking down her cheeks didn't match the twisted scowl of fury on her young face.

"FUCKING DIE!"

She screamed and the Legion Reapers before her ignited in flames. They cried out in surprise, trying to stamp out the fires with their also-burning hands as they whirled in panic. Their awful screams withered to silence as they toppled over, their flesh hissing and smoking in the Knight's rain until they were reduced to a heap of charred remains.

Avery almost froze, looking from the corpses to the young girl with blackened eyes. Cassie was one of Mona's witches.

A rain of arrows came from behind them from Lily, Shank, and Maria. Avery grew confident that they would be able to retrieve both Alice and Vinny's bodies as more Legion members combusted under Cassie's stare.

From the corner of her vision, she saw the younger Reapers freeing themselves from their burned ropes and Avery allowed herself to feel a small glimmer of relief. She didn't see the whistling projectile as it soared through the air and a sharp pain radiated through Avery's shoulder.

She looked at the arrow lodged beneath her left shoulder in confusion - had arrows even been coming from the enemy's lines? Her thoughts stumbled as she searched for a feather hanging from the arrow.

Why... why a feather?

She couldn't remember.

Avery swayed, teetering on her heels, the cold shock numbing the pain as fog clouded her vision and her legs crumpled underneath her.

– ✤ –

Moz could have sworn he saw the hot glow of fire from below the gaps in the cloud and instantly his worry for Avery grew. *Morgana.*

His chase with Peter became trivial once he knew that the Knights' ringleader was back down on the ground. The onyx Knight made a lunge for Moz's throat and his Knight rolled through the air onto its side, slashing at Peter with thick talons. When Peter reeled back, the Knight of Water launched back towards the ground to finish the demon of Fire.

He broke through the cloud cover and his stomach dropped when he saw that there was no Knight at all. *Who started the fires if not Morgana?* Through the Knight's eyes, he surveyed the battle scene for an explanation before he saw the feathered arrow stuck in Avery's chest. The next thing he saw was his world crashing down.

Down, down, we need to go down!

Moz hadn't expected the Knight to obey, but he found their shared body barreling back down to the earth. They crashed with hard impact, bones crunching under their talons as they landed without regard to the Legion Reapers below. Above him, Peter held back and launched back into the safety of the clouds. They were too large and too vulnerable to be in the direct line of fire from both sides but Moz didn't care anymore.

Gods, no, no, no, no, no!

The Knight roared out in fearsome warning and agony before clambering to cover Avery's body.

– 🕊 –

It took a long moment for Tristan to see the arrow lodged in the flesh just above Avery's heart and realize what had happened. It couldn't have been more than two inches beyond where she was protected by her chest plate. Such a narrow margin had such a deadly impact.

She sank to her knees and blood was rapidly seeping through the shoulder and front of her shirt. Her eyes were wide with horror before she toppled to the side and became a crumpled heap underneath her emerald cloak.

"AVERY!"

Lily shrieked her name, throwing down her bow to run to her friend and carry her out of the battle with both arms. Shank reached out their arm, trying to grab her by the wrist to keep her from running in the direction of the roaring Knight.

"Ya need to keep back!" Tristan drove his sword through a member of the Legion before chasing after her. "He doesn't care who y'are, he'll crush ya!"

The roar of the beast towering above them echoed in each direction before breaking into a rampage. With a toss of its head, teeth clamped down on the figure that had been running towards Avery to finish the job. The man's screams were silenced with the splintering crack of bones that Tristan heard even from the outskirts of the fray. He watched in horror as the Knight dropped the fleshy mess of a body back into the mud.

The Knight stood over her, its bony belly close above her body as though to serve as her skeletal shield while she laid on the ground. Lily ripped herself out of Shank's grip and ran ahead before the Knight turned in her direction and a wall of sound threw her braids behind her as a warning for her to stay back. Tristan grabbed her by the elbow and pulled her back to safety. He hoped that she was convinced of the danger and would listen.

"It's protectin' her, none of us will be able to get in," he yelled over the crunching of Legion bones as Moz kept snapping at all who still dared to approach Avery. "We have to wait!"

Shots rang out as a still-screaming Kurosaki picked off the Legion members with bullets, clearing a path towards Avery and Alice as he moved forward without regard to Tristan's warning.

The sapphire dragon suddenly imploded and Moz lay on his back yards from where Avery was bleeding. His bloodied body violently convulsed and Maria shrieked, running toward Moz.

"What in gods' names!"

Tristan ran to his side, examining Moz's face and gently slapping his cheeks. Lily ran to Avery's side, throwing her bow down to feel the pulse point on the side of Avery's neck.

"She's still alive," Lily called out, looking up at them in a plea for help.

"He's not conscious," Tristan looked up at Shank. "Pick Avery up as best y'can. Lily, go check the kids and help them carry the boy's body."

Tristan lifted Moz up when he finally went still, holding Moz's narrower frame over his back to carry him.

"What's happening to him?" Maria wailed with panic and she looked around at their faces for an answer.

Shank looked around for someone to help them lift Avery as Tristan caught Kurosaki's grief-flushed cheeks and blank expression, staring at Moz's limp body from where he kneeled over Alice.

"He's being Saved."

KNIGHT EXCERPT

The world around Moz was blindingly bright, each inch as far as his eyes could see was a sterile white. Beneath his fingers he felt a cool stone surface and he used the sensation to determine that wherever he was, he was laying on his back. His hand had been limp on his ribcage until he spread all his fingers on the floor to prop himself upright. Drunk dizziness overcame him and a blur of colors he did not notice before swirled in his vision.

Where am I?

He sat still for a long moment, becoming aware of the sweet whispers from somewhere around him. As he became steady his focus began to sharpen, the world came into view but became somehow more confusing.

It was in fact a white marble floor that he was sitting on and the black blur was the darkness of his own clothes as his lanky legs were laid out in front of him. An arcade of ivory columns formed a long hallway that he seemed to be sitting directly in the middle of. Beyond the arches were white stone walls, the frames of white doors could have easily been missed if Moz's assessment of his surroundings was any faster.

He rose to his feet slowly and another wave of dizziness threatened to put him back on the ground. Moz held out his hands before him to steady himself, straightening up only when he was sure that he truly did have his bearings.

"Hello?"

He was surprised by the cascading echo that followed and he looked up. Arcades upon arcades were stacked, the ceiling they led towards was much too far from the ground for Moz to see even with strained eyes. Where had he been before this place? Not even the Necropolis hosted such vast structures. Nervousness rattled his muscles and nearly convinced him to stay put.

Moz looked ahead of him and noticed the small splash of sky blue that seemed to be at the end of the hall. Was that the way out? He stepped forward, carefully at first before his stride hurried. The whispers grew louder as he got closer to the blue, realizing it was an archway leading outside. A small blur of red moved through the field of blue, was that a person?

After what felt like years, he finally made it to the entry to a large balcony, opening to the most incandescent sky he could ever recall seeing.

"At last, he wakens!"

He whirled around to see the small figure standing just beyond the archway. She could not have stood taller than Moz's waist and she smiled at him with the expression that could have only seen many years. The corset and skirts of her dress were wine red, the buckled belt around her waist matching the mahogany and brass boots that peeked out from under the asymmetrical skirts. Her golden hair was tied back in a braid that wound around itself many times, forming an odd sort of cone that bobbed on the back of her head and was anchored down only by the brass headdress she wore strapped around her chin. She looked up at Moz with dark eyes, heavy red makeup coating her eyelids.

"I did know that, however, didn't I?"

He didn't answer the question because it had only confirmed his recognition of the odd figure. Moz had seen it in illuminated manuscripts, in stained glass windows of temples.

"Neri, the Goddess of Oracles. That's you, isn't it?"

She didn't answer him either. Her face lit up and she turned around, shuffling hurriedly towards a bell that was fixed to the wall of the porch.

"There is no time at all for that! I must let the others know!"

She stood up on her toes, grabbing a gold and burgundy braided rope to swing it side to side. A sweet ring reverberated off the wall holding up the porch, seeming to echo off the lush white clouds. No sooner than it took for Moz to blink, he was surrounded by strange and fantastic people.

His eyes gravitated towards the figure in the center, bathed in the bright white that stretched tall in the vast hallway. The hood of her white cloak was gently draped over white tendrils of hair, the same shade on her lips and lashes. Her eyes, however, were the most brilliant shade of green and echoed the smile she regarded Moz with.

"Moz, my bravest son," she spoke and for a moment he was convinced his heart had stopped. He sank to his knees, overcome with adoration and devotion when it dawned upon him what was happening.

ACKNOWLEDGEMENTS

Hemlock was truly a team effort and I'd like to thank a handful of people for quite literally making this possible.

To my dearest mother: you bailed me out at the eleventh hour and nothing I write can express the gratitude I feel. I hope I've made you as proud as you make me.

To Heather, my beloved Stand-In Wife: thank you for all the times you came in to find me hunched over at my computer like a damn goblin and making me eat dinner. You kept me sane, or sane adjacent.

To Mary: your support and enthusiasm still amazes me every day and I don't know if I could have gotten this far without you in my corner. Thank you, thank you, a million times thank you.

To my congregation at Our Lady of the Earth and Sky: thank you for giving me a place when I needed to ground my feet again. You're all amazing people and your boundless love does so much for our community.

And thank you Mr. Rob Zombie, again, for the bitchin' writing soundtrack.

ABOUT THE AUTHOR

Elle Samhain is from the Seattle area and began writing *The Shintori Chronicles* while earning their Bachelor of Fine Arts at Washington State University. They are active in the pagan and queer communities, which have impacted both their writing and visual arts.

If they're not writing or making resin collages, they're probably binge watching *The X-Files* or talking to cats in sing-song.

Made in United States
Troutdale, OR
11/03/2023